DARKNESS

CREEPS

FORTH

This is a work of fiction. All of the characters, organizations, and events portrayed in this novel are either products of the author's imagination or are used fictitiously.

DARKNESS CREEPS FORTH

Copyright © 2014 by Brian Greiner

Published by Damn Fool Press
www.damnfoolpress.com

ISBN 978-0-9936983-0-9 epub
ISBN 978-0-9936983-1-6 mobi
ISBN 978-0-9936983-2-3 pdf
ISBN 978-0-9936983-3-0 trade paperback

First Edition : August 2014

This is for Lynn who encouraged me to write it, and Val who dared me to.

CHAPTER ONE

Excerpt From "The Book of the First Ascendant"

There is a darkness sweeping across our planet.

A darkness of the soul, fueled by all the petty hatreds and jealousies and greeds that lie within us all. But now these urges are being inflamed into monstrous life. Too many have embraced the rising darkness, battling for raw power, fueled by naked greed.

It is our purpose to be a light in the darkness.

It is our mission to lead Mankind to the Path of God.

CHAPTER TWO
The Sword Descends

The Doll S7H heavy equipment trailer rumbled heavily down Highway 401. Its load was carefully obscured with padding to disguise the shape, and with tarps to protect it during transport. Nothing, however, could disguise the HET but it looked similar enough to normal low-slung transports that it would not excite any interest to any but the most discerning observer.

Secrecy was the watchword for this trip. It began at CFB Petawawa and was to end at a heavy equipment shop in Quebec. The route was not the most direct of routes, but that, too, was part of the security plan. Designed by experts and approved at the highest levels, the plan for transportation of the cargo was considered flawless. It was vital that security be perfect, to avoid any political fallout. The Minister of Defense herself was adamant that no protest groups learn of the cargo much less the route.

The cargo in question was an enhanced 2A6M Leopard tank. An excellent tank, proven in battle, it was en route from testing by the Royal Canadian Dragoons. Rightly or wrongly, the tank had become a symbol for wasteful military spending by a government committed to overspending on big-ticket military items. With the purchase of a new fighter aircraft to replace the aging CF-18 bogged down with years of infighting and accusations of corruption, and the navy ship program grinding to a halt due to incompetent management, the Leopard tank upgrade program was the latest big-ticket item to come to public attention. To buy votes in Quebec, the government had ignored qualified firms in Western and Central Canada to give the upgrade order to an inexperienced firm in Quebec. Protesters of all stripes, from anti-war activists to budget waste protesters to anti-Quebec protesters to people just fed up with the whole venal collection of toadies and self-serving mercenaries in Ottawa, had zoomed in on this latest scandal-ridden boondoggle for all sorts of reasons. Oh, and national security played a small role in the security concerns, but only to the professionals. The politicians and bureaucrats were only worried about the protesters and political spin. Because of the overwhelming need not to draw attention to the trip the HET traveled alone with no escort, in the wee hours of the early morning to avoid traffic.

As the HET approached Highway 427, it suddenly signaled a lane change. It continued changing lanes until it was heading south on the 427. Surprisingly, this did not elicit any comment from Security Control who was monitoring the progress of the HET via a wireless communications link from the on-board GPS. This was, perhaps, not so surprising since the GPS and associated data link were actually on board a van that had been pacing the HET and was continuing eastward along Highway 401.

Soon the 427 came to an end and the HET continued eastward along the Gardiner Expressway. The HET was not seen as out of place, since with all the construction occurring such a transport was a common sight as they hauled large bulldozers and such from site to site.

As the HET approached downtown Toronto it began to gradually slow down, letting the sparse traffic pass it. Eventually it came to the Harbour Street exit, and it finally came to a stop with its flashers and tail lights strobing rapidly. A half-dozen men poured out of the cab and began slashing at the lines holding down the tarps, which were rapidly pulled off to reveal the Leopard within.

Suddenly, with a roar, the Leopard tank erupted into life. It spent a few seconds bellowing curses at the sky, then rolled off the HET and onto the roadway. From there, it accelerated down the ramp and onto Harbour Street. Picking up speed it turned north on Bay Street. Smoke began belching from the sides of the turret, and the *wumph* of the side-mounted mortars was heard at regular intervals.

A police car on a side street roared up with sirens blazing, but was quickly silenced by bursts from the 7.62mm machine guns.

As the tank passed Front Street, suddenly the main 120mm smooth-bore gun vomited with a roar of smoke and sound, and a split-second later the side of a building exploded into the night. Then another roar from the main gun and another building exploded. The main turret swung from side to side, periodically spewing destruction. The machine guns added a background chatter to the main gun, clawing away at buildings and vehicles.

Thundering past Wellington Street, King Street, Adelaide Street the guns of the tank raked destruction along either side of its path.

Onward past Richmond Street, then on Queen Street it slowed slightly as it jogged left then right and drove onto

Nathan Phillips Square in front of City Hall. The tank fired one last blaze of destruction into the middle of City Hall, then fell silent.

A brightly-coloured orange helicopter noisily clawed its way from the sky and landed in the Square, off to one side of the tank.

The top of the turret opened up and out came the black-clad crew of the tank. They scurried into the waiting helicopter and were whisked into the night. A fountain of flame erupted from the tank as the incendiary charges left inside ignited. An answering eruption of flame answered from the Gardiner Expressway as the HET burned as a result of similar charges.

The helicopter made a powerful leap upwards and made a quick flip to fly south as it rapidly gained altitude to rise above the smoke and haze of the destruction wrought by the tank. It continued flying south until it got to the lake shore, then banked, flew down towards the water, and was lost in the waiting darkness.

The city was silent for a moment.

Then the screams of broken buildings and broken flesh split the early morning darkness.

CHAPTER THREE
The Sword Speaks

"This is Melanie Goldsmith of AJF News."

"In breaking news, we have just heard reports of a terrorist attack on the business district of Toronto, Canada."

"Wait ... I have just been handed a bulletin."

"We have just received a communique from a group claiming responsibility for the Toronto attack. They call themselves 'The Sword of Infinity Ascending'. They say that the attack is punishment for economic crimes against oppressed humanity. They say that they deplore the necessity of violence, but that they have been forced to use extreme measures by the oppressive violence of the capitalistic exploiters. They further say that they regret any casualties but any such should be considered to be martyrs to the cause of economic justice. Economic justice will not be denied, and they will protect the interests of the people from capitalistic exploiters wherever the need is greatest."

"That is all the information we have at this time."

"This is Melanie Goldsmith, for AJF News. Stay tuned for further developments."

CHAPTER FOUR
Picking Up The Pieces

A small group stood around the smoldering remains of the Doll S7H trailer. A barrier had been placed around the remains, several meters back. The rearmost of the seven axles was embedded in the roadway, in what now looked like a sinkhole. Cracks radiated in all directions from the burnt-out husk, and the guardrail was shattered for the length of trailer.

"So who are we waiting for?" asked the representative from the fire department, "We need to get our people here to inspect the scene and check out the roadway. It looks in pretty bad shape from what I can see."

"The representative from the PMO should be here shortly," said the representative from the police department, looking resplendent in his full dress uniform. He was determined to show the PMO that the police, at least, were capable of showing proper respect for authority. "The PMO called the Mayor directly and insisted on an absolute but discrete lockdown of the affected sites. No media, no swarms of investigators, everything low-key with just enough of our people around to make it look like we're doing something but not enough to alarm people."

"Alarm people!" spluttered the military representative, "A tank just shot up downtown Toronto, for God's sake! We need to get a full response from everyone out here ASAP! We need heavy equipment to deal with debris and to search for survivors, not taping-off of the scenes! And we need to get our forensics people in to examine the tank and trailer to search for clues. We need to find the bastards that did this, not worry about political spin!"

A mousy-looking man interjected, "Don't forget the Ornge medical helicopter that was stolen from Saint Michael's Hospital! The theft of that puts a major hole in our ability to airlift trauma patients!"

He stuck out his chin and added, "And that's not even taking into consideration the replacement costs!"

The sound of a helicopter moving towards them rapidly grew louder and louder. It was traveling at high speed following the Gardiner Expressway, dropping lower as it got to the group. Within a few seconds it was on top of them, flaring up to kill velocity, then rapidly moving down for a landing. The engines whined as they powered down, and a door in the side opened up. A man exited, followed by a woman. They walked quickly and with deliberation towards the small group.

"My name is Higgins, and I'm from the PMO," said the man, "We're in charge here, now. All decisions for anything regarding this incident will go through us and us alone. Any contacts with the media will be made by us and us alone. You lot will do as you're told, when you're told. Any questions?"

The mousy-looking man determinedly stepped forward "Mr. Higgins, I'm Clarkson from the Ontario Disaster Response Unit. We appreciate your assistance, but this is a provincial matter."

"The hell it is," snapped Higgins, "This is a matter of

national security. Any interference with our authority will be treated with the utmost gravity, up to and including criminal charges. Is that clear? Now, where's the city works representative I asked for?"

A beefy man stepped up. "That'd be me. Name's Donaldson."

"OK, Donaldson," said Higgins, "I want your crews to get this mess cleaned up and disposed of ASAP. Take it all out to one of the hangers at the Downsview base."

"Uhm, OK, Mr. Higgins, sir, but we've got nothing large enough to transport anything this size, much less the tank. And the tank's all melted-like, too."

"Then use torches or cutters or whatever you need to chop this junk up into manageable pieces. Just get it out of here. By end-of-day tomorrow, at the latest," commanded Higgins. "Feel free to conscript the military for *any* assistance that you might require," he added with a glare at the military representative.

"Sir, I must protest," said the military representative in a shocked tone "It's vital that we find out who is behind this attack, and these wrecks are our only clues so far! We need our forensics experts to go over them!"

Higgins stepped up and glared sneeringly at the man. "Don't tell me what's important, you military dolt. It was you lot that was in charge of the transport operation, and you screwed up. Now it's up to me to put things to rights."

The military rep refused to back down. "No sir, it was the PMO who planned the route, against our advice. It was the PMO who overrode our decision to provide a full security escort. It was the PMO's idea to use a private security firm to perform the operation."

Higgins face grew cold and white with anger. "Don't contradict me you pissant little martinet. All your kind know is brute force. This operation required discretion and finesse to smooth over any problems with the protest groups and media. This government is dedicated to the principles of free enterprise, not boosting the empire-building aspirations of a bunch of ignorant tin soldiers."

With a visible effort Higgins composed himself. "This is how things are going to be done. The PMO is in direct control of this cleanup. Period. We have already invoked the priority override provisions for all telephone, cellphone, and Internet service providers for the duration. In practical terms that means that all communications bandwidth gets prioritised - government first of course, then business, and civilians get whatever is left over. We will control all information about this incident. We will control how people get this information. Only the official government media sites will have high-speed access for any civilians. Any other Internet access, and I mean ANY other access, will have its bandwidth throttled back to unusability. And that's the way it will remain until the site gets cleaned up to our satisfaction. The PM has an important meeting with international business leaders in just over a week, and he has guaranteed that it will be in Toronto. THAT is what is important gentlemen. Nothing will interfere with that. *Nothing*."

Higgins looked around the group and snarled, "Well, what are you all standing there for? Get to work!"

With that he stalked back to his helicopter. As he settled himself into his seat he sighed at the unfairness of it all, to be surrounded with such obvious incompetents. The wisdom of the PM`s decision to exert more control over all levels of government was becoming more apparent each and every day.

CHAPTER FIVE
The Mayor Speaks

"This is Zandra Faheed of AJF News, with an exclusive interview with Mayor Charles Fairstreet, the mayor of Toronto. Thank you for coming Mr. Mayor."

"Glad to be here, Zandra. Thank you for taking the time to come out and spend some time with me today."

"Mr. Mayor, our thoughts and prayers are with the citizens of Toronto in this time of terrible tragedy. Do you know the extent of the damage yet?"

"Thank you for your prayers, Zandra. I know that our faith and the faith of our supporters will help us through this terrible time. But to answer your question, no, we are still assessing the damage. Search crews are still combing the wreckage for victims of this senseless and cowardly attack. So far we've discovered the bodies of four victims in the wreckage, one more killed by machine gun fire, and of course the two brave police officers who died when their car was machine gunned as they responded to the disturbance."

"Mr. Mayor, I want to pause for a moment to show some footage that we took of you earlier today. Please interject with comments at any time."

A screen behind the Mayor and interviewer lights up to

show the Mayor wearing a hardhat and safety vest as he walks slowly surveying the wreckage. Federal disaster management officials can be seen pointing to this or that item of interest. The Mayor is seen nodding and looking alternately sad and concerned. The shots are carefully framed to show the Mayor looking taller than everyone around him.

"Yes, Zandra, it was heartrending to see the extent of the damage. As you know, several buildings in the business district were attacked, but the full extent of the damage isn't known. Those buildings will have to be closed for some time, I'm afraid, as officials fully assess the damage before allowing people back in."

The scene changes to show the Mayor carrying coffee to the search&rescue crews. Many are frankly annoyed at being interrupted for an obvious PR stunt, but the Mayor is oblivious to this as he walks around smiling and pushing cups of coffee into their hands. The scene shifts to show the Mayor picking up a small brick and carrying it to a nearby wheelbarrow. The effort seems to tire him.

"Mr Mayor, it is heartwarming to see how everyone, yourself included, is pitching in to help with the cleanup."

"Thank you, Zandra. I am pleased to be able to help in whatever small way I can. But it's not just me helping out, there are so many other volunteers working around the clock to support the cleanup and rescue efforts. I am truly humbled by the outpouring of effort."

"Mr Mayor, we're hearing reports that the roadway of the Gardiner Expressway is damaged to such an extent that even the support arches are damaged beyond repair. How will this be replaced?"

"Zandra, it's true that the roadway has been severely damaged. But this is a blessing in disguise! For years, decades even, the arguments have been raging about what to do with the Gardiner. My administration is taking the bold step of using this tragic occurrence and turning it into something wonderful. We are going to tear down the Gardiner. And I'm pleased to announce that the federal government has pledged funds from their new Infrastructure for Canada Program. This is truly a great project for the great citizens of the great city of Toronto."

"Excuse me, Mr. Mayor, but I must ask this. There have been some reports of protesters in the area, and of police arrests. Can you give us any insight into this?"

"Zandra, as much as it pains me to admit this, there are a few malcontents in our wonderful city who will take advantage of any opportunity to shame us all."

The scene on the monitor changes to show police dressed in riot gear, swinging their batons at a cowering crowd, before tossing them into transports and hauling them away. Only a couple of signs of any sort can be seen. Some of the crowd are wearing suits, some wearing casual clothes. Several can be seen clutching their bicycles.

"I want to personally thank our brave police officers for ensuring that the efforts of the rescue and cleanup crews are not hindered or mocked by these few malcontents."

"But Mr. Mayor, there are reports that many of those arrested aren't protesters, but simply people who work in the area."

"Zandra, I assure you that the police are being extremely careful in whom they arrest and using the absolute minimum force required to make the arrests necessary to secure the area. But in the unlikely case that an innocent person is detained, I assure you that the procedures that the police use to quickly and efficiently process each person detained will have any innocent parties released as quickly as possible."

"Thank you, Mr. Mayor. I'm sure that our viewers will

be reassured to know that law and order is being maintained in this difficult time."

"Zandra, if I may, I'd like to extend a special thank-you to the government's Canada News Centre team who came here from Ottawa to help us out. Their expertise in keeping the media informed has certainly been a big help to my staff, not to mention media representatives such as yourself."

"Yes, Mr. Mayor, they've been of immense assistance in helping us to get the facts out to everyone. But now we have to pause for a brief commercial message. When we come back, we'll have some international reactions to this horrible terrorist attack. Please stay tuned."

CHAPTER SIX
Cold Days

It was a cold, cold, cold day.

Cold as a senior bureaucrat's heart, and empty as a politician's promises.

Yancey Franklin walked along the Ottawa River on the way to his office, feeling the cold without and the emptiness within. His breath formed a cloud that trailed behind him like an airplane's contrail.

The day had started, as so many recent ones had, with Yancey feeling rather sorry for himself. Life as a private investigator was getting a bit thin. Thin in clients, and thin in interest. The rent for his apartment was coming up soon, as was the rent for his office. The usual clients that he depended on for part-time work simply weren't hiring these days. The 'economic slowdown' insisted on hanging on year after year, like a sinus infection that wouldn't go away. His savings were evaporating rapidly, but expenses refused to go away with the same rapidity. In fact, they had a nasty habit of growing.

Then he heard about the terrorist attack in Toronto, and suddenly his own problems felt pretty small. Major damage to offices in the financial district, and several cops killed along with some office cleaners, and other innocent bystanders. Some group of crazies had claimed credit for the attack, but their rationale made no sense at all. In terms of 'capitalist oppression' Bay Street was pretty small potatoes, and rapidly getting smaller. The attack seemed targeted at someone or something … hell, they used a frickin' *tank* to blow the beejeezus out of downtown Toronto. And how did they get their hands on the damn tank in the first place?

Yancey had friends who worked in that area. Jobs were scarce these days, and having one's place of employment obliterated by crazies wasn't exactly helpful. But his emails and phone calls to his friends were going unanswered due to overburdened communication systems that weren't up to the task. So many things were being built for 'average' use these days, and it was a rare day that 'average' occurred. Any emergency, however minor, always brought the phone and Internet systems to their knees.

He was especially eager to hear from Simon Thane, his best friend. Simon was working as a financial data analyst at a startup firm. It sounded like the building Simon worked in had been attacked, but it was impossible to find out any details.

Yancey glanced at his smartphone, but the 'message waiting' light remained stubbornly dark. The signal strength was fine, but the connection indicator kept flickering and was mostly 'off'. Given the situation, it looked like the government had invoked their service provider override provisions, and were grabbing all available bandwidth for their own priority communications.

What little information that was becoming available seemed to indicate a security and public relations disaster of epic proportions. What disturbed Yancey was that everyone, media and government, seemed more concerned about playing the 'blame game' than helping citizens to recover from the attack. Which meant that the 'priority' communications probably consisted mostly of PR firms and legislative staff madly scurrying around trying to put the best spin possible on the situation.

Yancey finally reached his office. It was a small office in a small, elderly business park that had seen better days. But those better days were a long time ago. He glanced at the small, tasteful sign on the door and sighed. He'd been so proud of opening up his own practice, 'YF Specialty Investigations'. But the sign was looking a bit worn, dated, and out of place. Much like he'd been feeling for a while.

"Ah, cheer up, ya fool" he thought to himself "Life's hard and then you die. Make the meantime a good time. Always look on the brighter side of life."

He continued chanting inspirational lyrics from favorite songs to himself as he went through the usual rituals of turning on lights, making coffee, and turning on his computer. His mood was improving when he started sipping on his coffee. It always did. And brightened still more as he realized that there was still one sugary pastry left from yesterday.

"Oh come to me, my sugary love," he crooned, "My waistline says 'no no', but my mouth says 'yes yes'."

He was halfway through the pastry when he noticed that the message-waiting light of his office phone was blinking. Hurriedly swallowing, he grabbed the headset and punched buttons to play the message. When he heard the voice of his friend Simon talking, a lump came to his throat. As Simon's voice quickly explained that he was fine, and everyone he knew was fine, another lump came to Yancey's throat. He'd been more worried than he realized. The message came to an abrupt end as the line went dead. While disconcerting, Yancey realized that it was just the overloaded phone system forcing an end to the call to allow a 'priority' call to go through.

Yancey thought furiously about how to contact his friend. He suddenly realized that as a registered business, his communications qualified for 'business priority' status, and a couple of his recent jobs had allowed him to acquire extra priority points. He'd originally cursed the government for pushing through legislation that allowed carriers to set up a tiered, prioritised (ie. overpriced and de facto rationed) system, but now he could use it to his advantage. Any real-time messaging over the Internet was out of the question for the time being, but email should get through fairly quickly, if he used up those brownie points.

He quickly composed an email to Simon, added his business identification number and special priority codes to the header, then fired it off to all of Simon's email accounts. One of those was bound to get through before the end of the day. He'd added enough information and pass codes for Simon to get higher priority when he replied, whether by phone or email.

With that done, he sat back in his chair and sipped at his now-cool coffee. But he didn't mind. Wheels had been set in motion and now all he had to do was wait. So he pecked away at his computer, and quickly discovered that access to any but official government websites was slower than molasses in the winter time. "Oh joy," he sighed, "Priority override at work. Making sure that we hear the official party line from the Prime Minister's Office before we get contaminated by reality."

He glanced at the government websites, but it became quickly evident that it was all about deflecting blame from themselves. Lots of pictures of some politicians making 'on site evaluations' and senior bureaucrats wearing vividly emblazoned vests doing 'sitreps', but no real information.

Yancey was about to log off in disgust, but stopped in mid-keystroke when a couple of pictures caught his eye. Behind the official government talking heads he saw what looked like police and non-official signs. Zooming in, he realized it was a police barricade holding back protesters. Not just rubberneckers, actual protesters with signs! He zoomed in as much as he could without blurring things too badly, and could barely make out some of the signs. Some said 'ECONOMIC JUSTICE', and some simply had what looked like the number '8'.

"Not much to go on there," he murmured to himself, "But my detective senses are beginning to tingle."

He thought for a moment, logged off, then stood up and stretched mightily. A series of subdued 'pop' sounds coming from his spine put a stop to that pretty quickly. "Time to get serious about shaping up," he sternly told himself as he wiped the last of the pastry sugar from his mouth while pointedly ignoring the somewhat rounded condition of his stomach.

The morning was looking up. Wheels were in motion, and there was an interesting mystery to look into. Although there were no paying clients involved, one can't have everything. But a detective needs information to sift through and his usual conduit, the Internet and its lovely databases, were out of reach for the time being. "Time to go old-school" he thought, and off he went to fetch some newspapers.

This was not as retro or foolish as it might appear. For a time it had looked like the Internet with bloggers and Wikipedia would eliminate newspapers entirely. And, indeed, many newspapers did disappear. But the survivors knuckled down, honed their craft, and made quality journalism a priority again. Then along came some complicated political scandals, and people realized that old-fashioned newspapers with their old-fashioned in-depth coverage of the news often trumped the Internet and its sound-bite bloggers. Improvements in printing technology to lower the costs, and better management software to reduce excess production costs, improved the economics to the point where newspapers could stop bleeding red ink. More importantly, newspapers figured out how to tweak their production and newsrooms to ensure that the current news hit the streets. All these combined to once again make newspapers competitive with bloggers and television news channels. Newspapers slowly became the go-to medium for quality reporting, once again. It also helped that many (but not all) of the newspapers weren't under control of the government. Any attempts to slap the same sorts of controls on newspapers that the government had put on Internet-based media were quickly met with strong legal resistance, and increased reporting of the appropriate official's misdeeds. People now tended to trust newspapers more than the other media.

A quick walk out and back had produced a half-dozen recent papers, all with some sort of coverage of the attack. Yancey sat down to do a more careful reading. As he read he began highlighting passages in different colours, and making notes on a pad of yellow paper. He liked making notes on paper. The scritching sound made by his pen, the tactile feel of paper, and the physicality of his movements all combined to intensify the information, and made it more 'real'. More importantly, it kept more aspects of his attention focused on the task, processing the raw data into something resembling useful information.

Equally important, the walk had also allowed him to acquire some food from Mama's deli. But he ignored the smell of the lasagna and the smooth flaky goodness of the pastry for a good half hour until he had completed a quick first pass of the papers. His 'detective senses' were still tingling, and somewhat more insistently. He absently reached for the lasagna, took an absent-minded bite, and chewed thoughtfully. The rush of flavours focused his attention on the lasagna. It was a bit on the cool side, but perfection is not harmed by a slight cooling, he thought. He ate quickly, but appreciatively. 'Mama' may have been an elderly Jamaican man, and despite being a confirmed heterosexual Yancey had on more than one occasion offered to marry him on the basis of his cooking alone. On those occasions, Mama's wife would laugh and offer Yancey a pastry, and Yancey would then beg for her hand in marriage. Or adoption. Yancey Franklin was something of a food slut, and knew it.

Mind and body thus refreshed, Yancey once again turned to the sprawl of papers and notes with a scowl. Then he glanced at his computer screen, which showed the official government web site. With a sigh he reached for a sheet of D-sized drafting velum, his preferred medium for drawing mind maps, and several pads of coloured sticky notes. He needed to figure out time lines, players, and connections. He hummed happily to himself as he worked, the worry over his friend temporarily pushed to the back of his mind.

CHAPTER SEVEN
The Spike

Herman Flagsworth loved his job. He'd hated it for a long while, but now the love was back. The thrill of the hunt, chasing down leads, pulling the pieces together. Oh, and the secret meetings with "unnamed sources", inside informants using dead drops to pass information (made so much easier these days with data keys) ... ah, this was like the good old days. Only better! This was the biggest thing he'd ever worked. The biggest thing he'd even seen, and he had seen a lot. After years of being sidelined doing the social page and human interest stories, this was going to put him back in The Game. Damn those damn kids and their damned J-school nonsense pushing him out of the way like he was some know-nothing hack. They knew nothing ... *nothing* ... about working a lead. To them working a lead was sucking up to a PR flack to get a bit of advance notice on a press release.

Herman had to admit that things had been changing for the better in the past couple of years, now that circulation was up. Some of the kids were actually willing to learn how to dig, and were developing a good nose for stories. Still, even the best of them still tended to patronize the Old Guard, who were the ones who kept the spirit of real investigative journalism alive during the Lean Years. And the worst of them, especially the ones in management, were utterly convinced that anyone over 30 was washed up. And Herman was over 30. Well over.

Internet bloggers were all the rage for while, even to the point where some people were predicting the end of staff reporters. Even the end of newspapers! Then the never-to-be-sufficiently-damned MBA-trained managers and their bean counter friends started to believe the hype, and the layoffs started. Then the shutdowns. Lots of good people got thrown away, and the decades of experience they had so painfully gained got lost with them. But enough newspapers clung to life to keep the tradition alive, albeit in a somewhat muted and mutated form. Then came the scandals, deliciously complex enough to require in-depth reporting by teams of experienced reporters. The bloggers couldn't match that! And the physical size of newspapers was ideal for laying out time lines and organizing the details like a story board. The bloggers couldn't match that, either!

Then came the telecomm wars, initiated when the federal government opened up the industry to all comers. "Let the wisdom of the market decide," they said. Hostile takeovers, foreign takeovers, and mergers were the result, all accomplished with enormous amounts of debt financing. Demand for bandwidth exceeded the supply, but no new infrastructure was being built out because the telecomm companies had racked up such large debts with their buyouts that they couldn't afford to build infrastructure. Then the feds stepped in with their 'priority override' legislation. To "enforce a sound market structure" on the available bandwidth "in keeping with national priorities", they set up a rationed access to bandwidth. And not just raw bandwidth, but also the priority of any communications. Government took their share off the top, then business, then taxpayers. The non-government users could improve their bandwidth and priority by paying an extra fee to the government. Most consumers didn't care if the movie they were streaming was delayed a few seconds, just so long as it got to them. But businesses were keenly aware of the effects of such latencies, and paid a great deal to minimize them. In addition to all this, the government slipped in a provision allowing them to grab bandwidth and data priority "in times of national emergency." In practical terms, the government rationed out the limited bandwidth to the highest bidder, but ensured that consumers got enough to get their music and movies without paying fees that were too onerous. In addition, the extra provisions allowed them to ensure that, when necessary, citizens saw only what the government wanted them to see. News organizations that played along with the government got better access to government officials and better bandwidth. This left a niche for the hard copy news organizations as the purveyors of unfiltered information. A new Golden Age for the newspapers.

One good thing about being old, Herman reflected, is that sometimes the people we knew as kids end up in interesting places, doing interesting things. And sometimes they remembered their old friends.

One such old friend had remembered Herman, and had come to him with an incredible story. His friend didn't have all the details, but had some hints about who might. And Herman was good at tracking things down, very good indeed. The more Herman dug into the story, the bigger and nastier it got. A truly major scandal. A game-changing scandal of the sort that brought down governments, invoked serious investigations, and ended up with important people in jail for a long time.

So Herman went to his editor, Charlene Blaverston. Younger than Herman, she was still Old School. Ah, the look on her face when he had pitched the story to her still brought a smile to his lips. First incredulity, then disbelief, then shock. Then hunger. Yes, she was definitely Old School to have that sort of hunger for a story.

Charlene laid down some pretty strict rules to protect everyone involved. No-one knew about it except the two of them. He alone was to know and keep all the details safe - he'd learned those lessons well in earlier times, and kept up with the latest digital techniques as the years went by. He was a pro of the Old School, after all. She was to be kept in the loop about the general thrust of the investigation. They set up a a system of code phrases and burn phones to communicate when they weren't in the office. Neither was unaware of the danger they were in, but they were investigative journalists of the Old School. They'd survived war zones and warlords. This was the sort of thing they did. Just not usually in their own country. This was definitely not the usual Canadian scandal.

Herman carefully typed up his notes on his desktop machine in his apartment, which was located in a good part of Toronto that was well-patrolled by the police. It was fully TEMPEST shielded, password protected, and encrypted. It was only plugged into his Internet connection when he absolutely had to, and even then he used a router and switch that were configured for security. The only way to attack was physically, and he'd taken precautions to deal with that. Or at least slow down any intruder long enough for the police to arrive.

Everything was stored electronically. Paper documents passed to him by his sources got scanned then shredded with a high-security shredder. Similarly, data keys and disks passed to him were scanned for malware, copied, then put through the shredder.

When he had to use the Internet with his desktop machine, he always used Tor to ensure both data security and untraceability. And he only used his desktop machine for this project.

At the end of every day (and sometimes more frequently) he put all the information onto a data key which he put into his safety deposit box. In addition, he had hidden backups in several places around his apartment. He'd even put one inside a live electrical box in the wall of his apartment, behind the plug. That one didn't get changed too often because poking around a live socket made Herman very nervous.

His data security was, in fact, top-notch. Charlene, although she didn't know the details of the data, had the necessary passwords to decrypt the data, if that became necessary. They had all their bases covered.

As the days went by, Herman kept adding to his store of information. Some of the stuff made no sense, and some was plain bug-shit crazy. But if it came along with the good stuff he added to the electronic pile. It looked as if there might be more than one big story there, but the main story was what truly demanded his attentions.

As information got collected, he began to arrange it into different folders. One for the main story itself and another for the corporate background information. The weird or crazy stuff got stuffed into a single folder until he noticed that it kind of fit into two general categories, so each of those got its own folder.

Everything was going so well, just like the old days. He had to dig like hell for each scrap of information, and he was so busy that he never questioned his good fortune at stumbling onto such a story.

Then one day Herman got his hands on another packet of information from yet another nameless source in yet another dark alley. It had been a very long time since he'd had to put in this sort of effort, and his age was beginning to show. He tossed the packet down and rubbed his face with his hands. Raising from his chair, he reached over to turn off the light on his desk and call it a night. The new pile of pages and data keys sat there accusingly. The habits of a long lifetime forced him back down to at least take a look. He settled down with a heavy sigh and started reading. Then he sat bolt upright and a feeling of cold ice ran up his spine. All thoughts of fatigue were gone, now, and he quickly read through the rest. Sitting back in his chair, he felt his hands quiver, and the rest of his body soon followed suit. Wrapping his arms around himself, his eyes teared up as he realized how far down a deadly rabbit hole he'd fallen. Herman had lived through the Cold War era as an investigative reporter, and had a very clear idea of the danger he was in. Lost though he was in fear, he realized that he wasn't the only one at risk. Charlene was in on this, too, but she didn't know about the worst of it. So he wiped his eyes and took a deep, calming breath. Then he began to carefully record all this new information, and update all his backups. He worked quickly but expertly, a calmness coming over him. Herman was a professional reporter, and the story would get out. If not by him, then by Charlene.

The next morning, Herman didn't show up at work.

That wasn't unusual in and of itself, but he hadn't alerted Charlene to his absence using one of their covert lines of communications. That was unusual, but not unheard of, so she didn't let her concern show. But when Herman didn't show up for work the next day, nor

27

contact her, she began to worry. So she made up a pretext to send a senior staffer (an old friend of Herman's) over to Herman's apartment with strict instructions to knock and then enter if there was no answer. She then waited impatiently for him to report back.

Charlene jumped a bit when her desk phone rang, and chided herself. She answered the phone and heard the voice of the staffer she'd sent to check on Herman. His voice breaking, he described how he'd entered the apartment to find Herman in bed, in his pajamas, dead. No signs of anything amiss, but he'd not looked around too much as he'd just called the police who told him not to touch anything. But he had peeked into every room and opened every closet, and nothing looked out of place. Charlene thanked him, told him to wait for the police, and to take the rest of the day off after he was done with them. Then she hung up. The only thing keeping the tears away was a cold feeling of dread in the pit of her stomach.

The police came, interrogated the staffer, then sent him on his way. They carefully looked around, took lots of photographs, then allowed the ambulance to take the body away for a full forensic analysis. Standard stuff in the case of an unexplained death when there was no obvious foul play involved. A few days later, the coroner released a verdict of "death by natural causes", in this case a heart attack. Nothing strange about a man of Herman's advanced years having a heart attack. The police sent someone out to look at the computer, and he found nothing untoward. There was nothing missing, no signs of anyone having been there for quite some time, and it was just an old man who had a heart attack in his sleep. Case closed.

Herman had no living family, and his friends were the people he worked with. So Charlene requested permission to take care of the funeral arrangements and the disposal of his personal property. Herman's lawyer knew that she'd been named executor of the will, so he made the necessary arrangements.

It was a simple funeral, but well attended. Herman knew lots of people, and many of them wanted to pay their respects. Surprisingly, or perhaps not so much, even some of the targets of his investigations showed up. One or two were there quite obviously to make sure that their nemesis was well and truly dead. Others were genuinely sorry about Herman's death. One of them explained tearfully to Charlene that although Herman was a real pain-in-the-ass (she had to smile her agreement to that) he was a pro, he played fair, and the world felt lesser for his passing. She had to agree with that, too.

Later, she went alone to Herman's apartment. She sat for a while on a kitchen chair, just looking around at the simple furnishings. Glancing down, she opened her purse as if to get something, then changed her mind and got up and started walking slowly around. Periodically she would glance into her purse. After making a complete circuit of the small apartment, she was reasonably sure that it was clear of any monitoring devices. At least the very expensive detector in her purse hadn't picked up anything. So she went over to the desk where the computer was and turned it on. As the police had mentioned, there was nothing abnormal about it. It was a standard installation of Microsoft Windows. She took a look at the various folders and their contents and had to agree with the police. This was an utterly normal and unremarkable computer. The only problem was, it wasn't Herman's.

She quickly got up and began checking all the hiding places that Herman had told her about, and found nothing. Before she could complete her search, there was a knock at the door.

She froze, not knowing what to do, her heart beginning to pound. Then she heard a male voice calling her name. It was an old friend, a police officer of long acquaintance. She slowly let out her breath, and taking a moment to compose herself, went over and opened the door.

"Hey, Jack," she said, "Nice to see you again! But what's a high-ranking officer like yourself doing in a place like this?"

She said the words with a bit of sass. She and Jack had shared a bed once, and only once, many years ago. That was back when she was still married. Jack had been too, although he was still married to the same woman. Though the brief sexual relationship had ended, a real friendship based on mutual respect had replaced it, to the surprise of both of them.

"Hey, 'Lene," said Jack, "Really sorry to hear about Herman. I heard that you were going to come by here, and I thought I'd check up on you. You doing OK?"

Jack's voice and attitude radiated genuine concern for his friend.

"Yeah. Just taking one last look around before I get it all packed up. The landlord is being an asshole about getting Herman's stuff out as quickly as possible so she can rent it out. I was just looking at his 'awards wall' - care to join me?"

"Sure."

They slowly walked over to a wall next to the computer desk. There were a few photographs of people, and few larger frames with yellowed newspaper clippings.

Charlene pointed to one group photograph "That was taken a couple years after Herman started working at the paper. If you look closely at the left-hand back row, you'll see a very young, very naive me. And that one over there was taken when Herman was posted to Moscow as foreign correspondent."

She pointed to each photo in turn and explained what it represented. There weren't too many of them, just enough for a man to remember special times. Special places. Special friends. Similarly the newspaper clippings represented special "firsts" that had meant a great deal to Herman.

"What's going to happen to all those pictures and things," asked Jack, "And those awards over on the bookshelf?"

"Well," said Charlene, "The photos and clippings will probably go to the Press Club. They like to keep that sort of stuff around. Inspires the newbies and brings back memories for the old farts. Like me, I guess. As for the trophies, I don't know. I think I'll display them at the paper for a while. That really would have embarrassed Herman, I think, but he would probably have enjoyed the chance to gloat over the 'damn kids' as he called them."

"When were you going to do the packing-up?" asked Jack.

"Oh, in the next day or two, I think," said Charlene, "Better to get it done sooner than later."

"That's good," said Jack, "That's good. Best to put it all behind you."

Something in his voice struck Charlene as odd. "What do you mean by that, Jack?"

"Nothing. Just that sometimes it's best to let what's in the past stay in the past. And not waste time digging around where's there's nothing to be found."

He paused for a moment then continued, "Well, anyways, I gotta be going. Just wanted to make sure that you were OK. You fine with getting back to the office on your own? I gotta get back to work."

"Why, surely, Jack. Thank you so much for dropping by to check on me. I have work to do, too. I'll just take a last look around, then shut off the lights. No need to wait for me."

After Jack left Charlene stood there, unsettled by her friend's remarks and tone of his voice. It was as if he was trying to warn her about something. Or away from something. She stood staring at the door for a long while, her thoughts darting about but circling around a growing and frightening suspicion.

"Oh, Herman. What the hell have we gotten ourselves into?" she whispered quietly.

CHAPTER EIGHT
The Lost Lambs Gather

It was an upscale establishment, close enough to Bay Street for its patrons to quickly reach with a brisk walk yet far enough away to give them a sense of taking a breather. Of course, now its location allowed it stay open despite the devastation just a block and a half away. Its patrons, normally the up-and-comers in the financial world, were increasingly adding 'former' to their beloved titles, as waves of layoffs swept 'The Street'. In the manner of their 'guild', they still hung out together to exchange whatever scraps of information they had. And commiserate about the loss of their position, or console the unemployed while silently thanking the fates for their own continued employment. The former were beginning to outnumber the latter.

The loss of physical offices was bad enough to warrant impromptu vacations to be ordered. What made matters worse was the loss of business that resulted from the shutdowns. On hold were services that arranged for financing and stock options, as well as accounting and auditing. The smaller establishments normally staked their name on their ability to quickly and efficiently process the business of their clients, but now all that was on hold until they could find new quarters, set up new equipment, and get everything set back up the way it was. Alas, time, tides, and business wait for no-one. In the current frantic environment of bids, mergers, acquisitions, and Initial Public Offerings, delays meant failure. Young companies need cash like humans need oxygen, and the resulting delays were beginning to affect their ability to raise capital, which in turn forced them to look for money elsewhere in a race to prevent collapse. Larger companies seeking to make bids for contracts suddenly found themselves without the capital to back up their bids, forcing them to withdraw until capital became available. All the affected companies were regrettably cutting their ties to the financial service companies, and that in turn was forcing the financial service companies to scale back. And in some cases to close up shop completely. Hence the rising tide of unemployed young masters-of-the-universe.

Simon Thane sat at his usual spot and listened to the buzz of the crowd. Some people liked to run the feed from Twitter through fancy sentiment analysis programs, but in his opinion that was a sign of pure laziness or an unhealthy infatuation with technology. The financial business was about people dealing with people in a face-to-face manner. Besides, tongues loosened in places like this, and not just from the alcohol. Rivalries that were important while at the office receded a bit when everyone was here, and the camaraderie of the industry exerted itself. It was very common for people to move between companies. Not exactly like mercenaries, although a few viewed themselves in that way, but there was a certain loyalty to the profession as a whole that transcended any single company. The fact that more of those companies were treating their staff like interchangeable expendable widgets that existed for the benefit of the owners certainly contributed to that camaraderie all the more.

What Simon picked up was both heartening and disturbing. Disturbing in that it sounded like more people were joining the ranks of those on 'indefinite unpaid leave' or outright laid off. Heartening in that the inherent camaraderie of the industry was strengthening with a stronger sense of community being developed. Being one of those who genuinely enjoyed working as part of a team, Simon approved of the increased community spirit. It made things a lot more fun. On the downside, he and his coworkers were amoung the ranks of the unemployed. In fact, he was waiting for his former office-mate to show up, and she was running late. So Simon sipped his beer and waved at familiar faces, and bought a beer for those who needed it but were afraid to spend the money on another. It's not that he was profligate with his money, but rather that he was a great believer in helping out his friends.

It was as he was sipping and waving that he felt rather than saw someone slip into the seat beside him. He turned and smiled as he saw that it was his office-mate, or rather former office-mate, Gretchen Sinclair. He feigned shock and horror as she reached over, grabbed his beer, quickly drained half of it, then passed it back into his hands. "Ack! Ack! Girl germs!" he protested. Gretchen rolled her eyes in disgust and sneered, "Gah! You idiot!"

But her eyes twinkled even as she glared at her former coworker. This was standard fare for these two, but some things never get old.

"Well, if you were paying attention to your surroundings instead of undressing the waitresses with your eyes you'd have noticed me when I walked in. So serves you right for not having a beer ready for me, boy-o," said Gretchen primly. Simon laughed as he drained the remains of his beer and signaled for a pitcher of beer and another glass. Both arrived within seconds.

"Uhm," started Gretchen, "Shoulda asked me before ordering. I can't stay too long - got a hot date tonight."

Simon arched an eyebrow but was otherwise nonplussed. "No alcohol will go unconsumed in this crowd, so no worries on that score. So who's the lucky lady? Anyone I know?"

"Like I'd tell you," Gretchen sneered, then her demeanor softened. "Please promise me that you won't kill the pitcher on your own,"

She was no prude, Simon knew, and had no problems with people have a drink or three, but seeing anyone drink uncontrollably seemed to pain her at a fundamental level. She was a bit embarrassed by her show of concern so she hurriedly continued, "What's the buzz tonight? Any juicy tidbits?"

Simon told her about his impression of the crowd's mood, and then happily began relaying the tidbits of facts, rumours, and rumours of rumours that he'd heard. He'd sensed that her mood was a bit "off", so he pitched it as somewhat on the light side. As he rattled off the news, he watched her face. Normally he could jolly her out of any down mood, as she could him, but tonight she was not to be jollied. Her mood became pensive, and she began nodding with each new piece of information he gave her, as if she was crossing it off a list. He'd seen this 'list crossing' behavior before, and it typically meant that she had focused her keen analytical mind on some problem and was using the new information to confirm her analysis. It was was part of what made them such an effective team - he was good at teasing out information from a sea of raw data, and she was good at integrating that information into a larger whole. They'd been thrown together by the whims of fate, and despite a rocky beginning they had learn to believe in and trust each other for the better part of 5 years. Each very much missed the daily interplay of that teamwork.

Finally Gretchen sighed and took a sip of her beer. "Damn," she said, "It's worse than I thought."

Simon was puzzled, as what he'd told Gretchen about their little community shouldn't have surprised her that much. Then she started telling him about the things she had heard. About the small companies being forced to sell out to larger companies because their IPO or source of funding had dried up. Companies forced to withdraw bids from major projects. About how the interest charged for corporate financing was now going up. Then she dropped her bombshell. The newly-created National Securities Regulator, the first-ever attempt to create a national regulator that would replace the patchwork of provincial regulators, was now dead in the water. The computers, and more importantly the data, was destroyed.

"But what about backups?" queried Simon.

"Remember the to-do about the cost and how the government promised to eliminate waste?" asked Gretchen. Simon nodded, with a sinking feeling in his stomach. "Well," she continued, "It turns out that all backups were made and stored on-site. The blast that took out their office also took out all the backups."

Simon was dumbfounded. "No, wait a minute ..." he began.

"No," Gretchen interjected, "This is gospel, not rumour. The NSR is will soon be officially canceled. With no office and no equipment and no data, they'd have to start from scratch. Remember the cat fights that took place when it was created? The provinces haven't forgotten those, and several have said flat out that they won't go through that again. Worse, the talks to reduce or eliminate trade barriers between the provinces have been canceled because of the overheated feelings re-establishing the NSR has created. And there's talk by some provinces of setting up official tariffs and duties for inter-provincial transportation of goods."

"What?" spluttered Simon, "Those talks are *essential*! They've been overdue for years, decades even. Hell, as things stand right now, it's often cheaper to deal with companies from outside the country than companies in a different province! Adding duties on top of that is freakin' insane! Your sources must be wrong about this. They *must* be."

Gretchen shook her head. "This little tidbit comes straight from The Pipeline."

Simon fell silent at this. The Pipeline was rarely wrong, and never over something of substance. He didn't know who or what The Pipeline was, and he had never pressed Gretchen about it. It was something that she shared as one friend to another, and Simon would never betray that confidence.

"I'm meeting The Pipeline later tonight," Gretchen continued, "And in fact I gotta boogie right now."

She stood up, drained her glass, and punched Simon lightly on the shoulder. "Hang in there, bucko," she said softly.

"Yah, we're all in this together," Simon joked, then he watched her leave. His mood was, if not dark, then distinctly unhappy. Then some colleagues wandered by and noticing his glum expression, proceeded to regale him with dirty jokes of increasing impossibility until he laughed so hard his sides started aching. He shared the pitcher of beer with all and the gang moved along, leaving Simon sitting there happily thinking his own thoughts.

A short time later he felt a light buzzing coming from

his smartphone. He looked down and saw that he had got a message from his friend Yancey! Hot damn, he thought, service must be getting restored. He opened the message and saw the priority codes in the header. He was embarrassed and touched to see how much money and 'karma points' his friend was spending to get in touch. Not to mention surprised at the high priority levels. Those levels weren't just tossed around. His friend must have helped out someone important! Best of all, the priority included authorization for a return message! Simon quickly read the message, then composed and sent one of his own. The increasingly raucous sounds around him, and the contact from his best and oldest friend, served to lighten Simon's soul considerably. He took a deep breath and let it out slowly while picturing the path of a Celtic knot, a trick that Yancey had taught him. Life was good.

* * *

Gretchen got out of the taxi and walked towards the motel room that she'd booked earlier that day. It wasn't the first time she'd played this particular game, and it had always ended joyously for both parties. This time sounded different, though. More serious, and less playful. What the hell, she thought, there ain't no serious that can't be dulled with a bit of friendly play. Her curiosity mingled with anticipation as she approached the door, unlocked it, and entered.

"Hello, Gretchen," said Charlene Blaverston, "I'm glad you're finally here. I didn't know who else to turn to."

And with that the two women embraced.

Gretchen's excitement turned to concern as the older woman's embrace turned into something akin to being held by a drowning person. And concern turned into outright worry when Charlene began sobbing into Gretchen's shoulder.

This was a surprising turn of events, since it had always been the older woman who had held and comforted Gretchen over the years. They had met over a decade ago, when the winds of social change had made Canada a safer place for non-heterosexuals. Gretchen had been new to Toronto, with half-healed emotional scars from a lifetime of living in an environment of fear, repression and guilt. Loneliness had driven her to the bar scene in an attempt to feel at least the illusion of camaraderie, and luck had landed her in a 'safe bar'. Charlene had seen her there, alone with her fear and misery. The older woman knew all too well what that lost look and body language meant, and struck up a conversation. She wasn't looking for a hookup or any sort of relationship at all, but she was damned if she could stand by and not help. As a reporter she'd seen too many hurt souls that she couldn't do anything for, and knew that often a friendly word went a very long way.

So they had talked. Not about anything in particular or terribly personal, but as one friend to another passing the time of day. Each found the other easy to talk to. They shared a similar sharp, inquiring intellect leavened with a view of the world that was in equal measure caring and cynical. The older woman made sure that the younger knew about the safe places in town, agencies to call, that sort of thing. That was the first night of many. Over the weeks they became friends, though neither was the sort to make friends easily. Some months later, despite their best intentions, they became lovers. They both meant it as a one-time thing, but instead it became an enjoyable part of their friendship. As time passed, they realized that there were too many differences between them to make the relationship a long-term commitment. But their deep respect and friendship survived that knowledge, and they kept in touch through the years. Usually getting together to gossip and share tidbits of information, but occasionally to enjoy a more intimate encounter. Old friends fully sharing themselves as comfort against an often cold world.

In recent years, however, a change had come to the social matrix of the country. A change came to the federal government, especially after the creation and election of the Conservative Reformation Party. It started as a rigid economic fundamentalism, but quickly exposed itself as something more harsh and far-reaching. One piece at a time, the official attitude to 'deviancy' hardened. No laws were passed, or broken, but the interpretation of laws and regulations steadily favoured the so-called 'old fashioned' values. This harshness and narrowness began to filter down to the provincial and municipal level as progressive governments fell and non-progressives were elected. The progressives had only themselves to blame, of course. They became too quick to hop onto bandwagons of the 'cause du jour', too quick to exclude and mock any who dared to question their causes in even the slightest way, and far too quick to make expedient decisions for the sake of those causes. Moral certainty gave way to arrogance and a sense of entitlement. Fiscal management and good governance became something to scorn, as did the generation of new ideas that might upset the status quo. New political forces arose to oppose the greed and corruption of the established powers, and the voters threw out the morally and ideologically corrupt parties that had once been the leading lights of progressive thought. The new political masters, alas, proved to be even more dogmatic and narrow than the old ones. But now there was little in the way of organized opposition, as the progressive parties fought amoungst themselves over who to blame for their downfall. And so the regressive forces continued to rule, and tighten the screws against any who refused to walk in their narrowly-defined path.

Charlene and Gretchen, as did most others, learned to weather the storm. They learned the ways of discretion and misdirection. Their careers were going well since both were intelligent, talented, and had gotten started before the repression began. As Charlene rose in the ranks of her profession, the information that she passed on to her young friend revealed more of the inner workings of Gretchen's profession. This passing of information wasn't strictly one-way, of course, and each profited by the exchange. The information passed never broke any laws or confidences, for neither woman would never have abided that for an instant. And every once in a while they found the opportunity to exchange more than mere information, to the delight of both.

Which explained why Gretchen was so shaken by her older friend's reaction. Charlene had always been the rock, the strength, the wisdom of the young woman's world. Although startled by the turn of events, Gretchen carefully soothed her friend. She managed to get them both sitting on the bed, and Gretchen continued to speak soothingly, as if to a frightened child. Charlene eventually regained control of herself, and pushed away from Gretchen. Brushing the tears from her eyes, she stammered out an apology.

"Hush, woman," said Gretchen sternly, "We've been friends too long to apologize for tears! Besides, how many times have you dried mine over the years? It's about damn time I was able to return the favour!"

Although her tone was light, Gretchen was beginning to feel frightened. Charlene was strong and tough, so whatever had gotten to her this badly had to be very ugly.

Slowly Gretchen teased the story out of her friend. She'd heard about the death of Herman Flagsworth, but Charlene had told her not to come to the funeral. She already knew about Charlene's relationship with Jack, of course, but not that he'd seen Charlene at Herman's apartment. What she didn't know was that Herman and Charlene had been working on a very big story together, one that required the strictest of precautions to be taken. Charlene hesitated at this point in the telling. "Gretchen, you can walk away at this point. At least, I'm pretty sure you can. Herman was murdered. I'm sure of it although I can't prove it. That means I'm probably in danger, too, though only Herman knew the details. I probably shouldn't have met you tonight but ..." and she began to cry again.

Gretchen stiffened. No-one threatened her friends. No-one. Not ever. She knew that her friend sometimes swam in deep waters, and had probably stumbled onto a secret that someone wanted kept hidden. That didn't matter. She cradled the older woman's face in her hands and gently kissed away the tears. "I've already figured out that it's about bad people trying to do bad things. But they don't know who they're dealing with, my love. Together we'll figure something out. We always have. And if it comes to it, I know people that can help."

The last was probably something of an exaggeration, but right now she was going to say anything to help her friend regain her self-control.

"You don't understand!" whispered the older woman intently, "This is just about the biggest and worst scandal in Canadian history! And it's going to get worse before it gets better. A lot worse."

Charlene had no more tears to cry at this point, and her

face had a haunted look that tore at Gretchen's heart. Someone was going to pay for this, she swore to herself.

Gradually Gretchen teased the story out of Charlene, and the older woman was not exaggerating in the slightest. One of Herman's numerous contacts had leaked a hint about a scandal. Being an old pro, and one with something to prove, Herman followed up and confirmed it. The federal government had been pushing for electronic voting machines and Internet voting for some time, and had managed to set it all up just before the last election, which had been hotly contested. What Herman found out was that the voting machines had come from American companies, and those same machines and software had a history of flaws being exposed by security researchers. With those flaws supposedly corrected, the Canadian government had ordered enough of them to be placed in all but a handful of voting stations. What Herman found was proof, real proof in the judicial sense, that at least some of the new machines and Internet voting software had been compromised. Enough to affect the election. Herman had names, dates, everything. And he'd promised a lot more to come as one lead led to another. But Charlene didn't know the details, because of the security arrangements that she and Herman had set up. Then Herman died of 'natural causes'. Yet his computer had been not just wiped clean of his research data, but replaced to show a totally benign setup, something generically suitable for a man of Herman's age.

"And," Charlene added, "All of the backups that Herman had secreted about his apartment were gone. Except this one."

With that she reached up her skirt, fumbled for a moment, then pulled out an ordinary-looking data stick. She took Gretchen's hand and placed the data stick into it.

"That's the emergency backup stick. Herman hid it inside a wall socket behind the socket fixture. It was a real pig to get at, and Herman always had a bit of phobia about electricity. Don't know why. The old fool would go anywhere and do anything for a story, but he was afraid to so much as change a light bulb."

Her eyes teared up as memories of her old friend rushed unbidden to mind. "After Herman's murder, there's no-one at the paper that I feel comfortable going to about any of this. And I had to talk to someone, and ... and ..."

She stumbled into an embarrassed silence.

Gretchen looked at the data stick in her hand as if it was going to explode. "Uhm, uhm," she stalled, "Uhm you talked about uhm security. Wouldn't he have, you know, encrypted it or something?"

Gretchen hated sounding like a flustered schoolgirl, especially in front of Charlene, but her mind was reeling as probability trees and systems of consequences unfolded before her. That was what she did, and she was very good at it, but she couldn't always turn her ability off.

"Yes, of course, dear," Charlene spoke softly, "And I've got passwords galore from Herman, and I will give you those, of course. But I'm not sure really how to use them properly. Herman gave them to me, and gave me a quick-and-dirty course on how to use them, but he never thought to give the necessary programs, figuring it was all self-evident, and you know that I'm not altogether comfortable with computers."

Gretchen nodded, smiling. Her friend was brilliant, but her computer abilities maxed out at doing emails and web searches. "That's OK, love," Gretchen assured her friend, "You know I'm better at this sort of thing than you are! That's what friends are for, isn't it? Anyways, whatever I can't figure out, I know someone who can. And he's a security whiz, too. And a private investigator, to boot! Don't worry, my dearest love, we'll get it done!"

And with that she tenderly held her friend, as a mother might hold a frightened child. Her words and manner were soft and soothing, but the look in her eyes was cold steel with the promise of fire.

CHAPTER NINE
Speaker For Infinity Ascending

The darkened room was quiet. The furnishings were of the finest quality, but none of those in attendance noticed. The food and refreshments were of the highest quality, but none were partaking. Everyone's attention was focused on the centre of the table where a plain speaker-box sat, like a simple shrine. Suddenly a light on the small box glowed.

"This is Apostle One, speaking for Infinity Ascending."

All present jerked upright as if jolted by an electric shock. Their demeanor was focused, their eyes were brightly alert.

"It is time to receive reports as to the status of your current assignments. Place your data chips into the receptacles on the speaker-box."

Quickly and efficiently, as if from long practice, hands reached forward to insert their data chips. All motions were firm and steady, without hesitation. There was a rapid blinking of lights on the speaker-box.

"I receive your reports with thanks. The information will be processed and you will be contacted if there are any questions from me."

No sound escaped from those assembled, but the level

47

of tension was diminished by a fraction.

"Hear the words of Infinity Ascending and attend to orders."

The level of tension immediately rose, and all leaned quietly forward.

"At the next meeting of the Bilderberg Group the following items will be attended to. A list has been sent to each of your data chips of the companies that are to be acquired and by whom. The list also indicates the companies that are to be bankrupted and by what means. Acceptable time frames are indicated for each action. Members whose fortunes are inconvenienced by these actions will be compensated in due course. Progress reports will be expected, and are to be sent to Apostle Three via the usual secure channels."

One of the seated members raised his hand. The voice acknowledged the questioner, who asked "What about the members of the Skull and Bones Group? This will be impacting some of them. Making changes of this magnitude will be difficult or impossible in light of their certain resistance."

The questioner then fell into a respectful silence.

The voice responded "An excellent question, but this will not be an issue. The Skull and Bones Group has been brought into our fold. They have been informed of what is to occur. There will be no challenges from them."

That announcement caused those seated to break discipline and murmur in astonishment. Tensions between the two groups had exploded into hostile action on more than one occasion.

The voice paused for a moment to let the information sink in, then continued "These are the orders of Infinity Ascending. This communication is ended."

And with that the box turned dark. In contrast, the

mood of the room brightened as eager hands reached for their respective data chips. Wheels were in motion. The Great Game was in play, and all were eager to do their part and claim their share of the spoils.

CHAPTER TEN
View From The Shattered Palace

Colonel Frederick Brown was not a happy man. This was not, alas, an unusual condition. In truth, he had a lot to be unhappy about. He was the Senior Canadian Officer of the base, but his superior officer was an asshole. Worse, he was incompetent. Col. Brown could forgive the former, but not the latter. To put the icing on the cake, said superior officer was a foreigner, specifically an American. A proud and capable people, in Brown's option, but their leaders tended to transform that into arrogance and a hubris based on other people's accomplishments. His superior officer, General Thomas Thansworth the Third, took those qualities to new heights by adding incompetence and a total lack of self-awareness to the mix.

Col. Brown sighed heavily in the privacy of his own quarters. Such a glorious end to a mediocre career, he thought as he looked around his palatial accommodations. The 10-foot by 10-foot room wasn't so bad, he supposed, especially compared to the cramped quarters endured by naval officers, or by his subordinates. And the furnishings made it efficient enough to get the job done, all in all. No, it was the peeling bilious green paint that truly highlighted the disapproval he had with his quarters. That and the sweating pipes with flaking insulation that criss-crossed the ceiling. Oh, and let us not forget the smell, he thought to himself. The smell of decades of crushed hopes and the sour stench of desperation denied surcease. Such a lovely place to end one's career was the Shattered Palace.

Brown got heavily to his feet and walked over to the full-length mirror to check his appearance. Appearances counted for a lot, in a duty station like this. The troops thought him something of a martinet with his fussy attention to personal details. But Brown knew that it was the little things that mattered in an isolated end-of-road posting like this. He'd seen what happened when military personnel stopped caring, and he wasn't going to let that happen here. Let them hate me, he thought, just so long as it stops them from hating themselves. They were good troops, all in all, he thought, and it just their bad luck that saw them exiled here.

The image in the mirror looked back at him with a baleful expression. A quick shake of his head turned it into the basilisk gaze of a Colonel in the Canadian Armed Forces. He had learned at least that much in his career, even if he'd never quite got the hang of not speaking truth to power. He did a quick check of his uniform and finding no fault, he spun on his heels and exited out into the corridor.

The corridor was, if anything, seedier than his quarters. He knew for a fact that it had been painted just a few years before, but paint couldn't hide the age and general decrepitude etched into the bones of the facility. As he walked toward the Control Room, he crisply returned the salute of everyone he encountered. Their salutes ranged from half-hearted to quite vague, but he used the opportunity to silently remind them of their military heritage.

The base was quite compact, and it took very little time to arrive at the Control Room. His second-in-command, Major Jean Frontenac, saluted and handed Brown a folder. "Sir, here's the background information on the disciplinary panel for this morning."

Col. Brown stifled a groan. He'd managed to forget all about that. This was just the sort of thing that was going to happen when men and women got thrown together in an isolated base that was a career dead-end. Especially when most of their fellows were on their last tour ... the 'Last Leggers'. He couldn't blame them, really. Both were, if not young, then not quite middle-aged, and single. No harm, no foul. Except that military regs were quite explicit about this sort of thing. Why couldn't those two idiots keep things a little more discreet? He'd already been forced to reduce both of them by one rank. And General Thansworth was beginning to think that a general Court was the best way to handle this, to make an example out of them and put the fear of God into the rest of the troops. Damn, but TwoTee was such a royal pain. Damn again, he had to stop using that silly nickname that the troops has given to the General, even to himself. One of these days he was going to slip up and use it, like many of the troops already were. He'd had to take official notice of their use of it and discipline them for it, so he'd damn well better not start doing it himself. He made himself take a deep breath and slowly exhale. "We'll see them in Wardroom 2," he told Frontenac, taking the file and slowly walking to the room in question. He didn't need to look at the file's contents, as he already knew it by heart.

Brown and Frontenac walked the short distance to the wardroom, and saw two soldiers braced to attention outside the door. "Inside, the both of you," growled Brown as he entered the wardroom. The small room was sparsely furnished, with a pair of chairs and a small desk. Both he and Frontenac sat down on the chairs behind the desk. The two soldiers entered crisply, came to attention in front of the desk, and saluted.

"Corporal Douglas Fleming, reporting sirs!" said the first, saluting.

"Private Molly Landry, reporting sirs!" said the other, saluting.

The two officers maintained a basilisk gaze upon the offenders, letting the silence lengthen uncomfortably. Brown finally returned the salute and said, "Stand at ease."

The two soldiers relaxed only slightly.

Brown turned his gaze from one to the other before speaking. "You both know why you're here. It's the same damn thing as before. I've given warnings, I've busted the two of you in rank, and you're both still too stupid to be even the least bit discrete about your affair."

The two soldiers were somewhat disconcerted by the bluntness of the statement, but were trying not to show it.

The male soldier opened his mouth to speak, but closed it before any sound could come out. The female soldier stared resolutely straight ahead.

"OK," said Brown, "Here's how it's going to be. You WILL cool it for a while. No, stop looking stubborn, I'm serious. The General is on the warpath and is sorely tempted to make an example of the two of you. You're both young enough to think that a Courts Martial can't hurt your lives at this point, but I'm here to tell you that you're very, very wrong. You think that the Shattered Palace is the ass end of nowhere. That it is so far down the hole that nothing matters any more. Well, you're wrong. You'll both be out of here eventually, and I know damn well that you'll be leaving the military when that happens.

You will be wanting a clean record when that happens, trust me on that. You won't be able to get a job without one. So I'm begging you, cool it for a couple of weeks and for God's sake be more discrete after that!"

Brown's scolding had started sternly enough, but by the end there was a distinct pleading note to his voice.

The two soldiers were flabbergasted. They'd entered the hearing resentful about their careers, their lives, and the whole idiot system. Now here was an officer, a Colonel of all people, pleading with them in an obvious attempt to help them. They knew Col. Brown was a real stickler for the rulebook, and although he had always attempted to protect his troops from the General's stupidity, this was the first time they'd heard him plead with anyone.

"Yessir," gulped Cpl. Fleming, "We're sorry, sir. We really are. It's just ..."

"Sir, we really are sorry to cause you trouble, sir," began Pte. Landry.

"Enough," snapped Brown. Then his voice softened somewhat, "Look, you're young and single and isolated in the middle of no-where. Fair enough. But we're still Canadian soldiers doing a vital, necessary duty. You are both talented technicians, with a future ahead of you when you leave the service. But I cannot overlook this latest breach of military discipline. It will be noted in your permanent records. You are both docked one day's pay. Dismissed."

Both soldiers came to parade attention and saluted crisply. Brown returned the salute with equal crispness, and the two soldiers spun on their heels and marched out of the office.

Major Frontenac turned to his superior officer and said, "The General won't like this. He wanted blood."

Colonel Brown turned to his subordinate and said

coolly, "This is a Canadian facility, at least nominally. We are Canadian soldiers, and I am the Senior Canadian Officer. As such, responsibility for maintaining discipline amoungst Canadian troops falls to me and me alone. The General is responsible for overall base operations and the American contingent."

"Yessir," agreed Frontenac, "But he'll destroy your career if you don't do what he says."

"This is my last posting," Brown replied, "And it'll end by the end of the year no matter what the General thinks or wants or does. My duty is to my Country and to those under my command, not to some foreign general."

"Yes, SIR!" said Frontenac smartly.

Col. Brown sighed briefly then continued, "Let's do the rounds before heading back to the Control Room."

As the two officers walked through the facility, Brown found it hard to keep his thoughts from the vast snowy expanse of forest that existed outside the facility. To his mind, the vastness of the vista and purity of the air allowed a person to simultaneously be at peace with the world, and to give enough space for one's soul to transcend itself and encompass the world. For him, it was the quintessential Canadian experience.

The echos of their footsteps in the decaying corridors brought his mind back to the here and now. Brown and Frontenac walked down each corridor. They went to, and examined, each of the three portals and their doors that controlled access to the outside world. They walked down the main corridor, curving as it did past the cafeteria and common room. They entered the common room to draw a cup of coffee. Sipping it carefully, Brown decided that the last shipment of coffee was as distinct improvement previous shipments. Still not up to standard, but better than the crap that they usually got. He was very careful to ensure that he partook of the same food that his troops got, with no special treatment. The General was not so careful.

The room had fallen silent as the two officers entered. Seeing the two of them quietly drink their coffee, conversation slowly got back to normal. The two officers carefully took no notice of the conversations, but keenly observed the morale of the soldiers.

Finishing their coffee, they got up, put their mugs into the appropriate tray, and continued their rounds. The next stop as they walked the curve of the corridor was the computer room. Here they stopped as the two officers looked into to the window to gaze at the faded high-tech glory of decades past, now thoroughly obsolete and barely operational. Which was quite all right, since there was little of any relevance for it to do. And that explained the sight of the two computer operators, sitting at a desk intent on their usual game of Dungeons and Dragons. Somehow the pen-and-paper game fit in with the tenor of the room. Besides, all electronic devices were strictly forbidden within the Shattered Palace for security reasons. Not a bad rule, thought Brown, but it certainly added to the strain felt by all of them. He felt sorry for the computer geeks, though. Recruited by the Forces for their technical know-how instead of physical prowess, they had almost completed Basic Training when their geeky instincts got the better of them. Although the pictures they posted were embarrassing instead of scandalous, they were of an officer whose family connection reached very high up indeed into the corridors of power. Outrage was clearly communicated and action demanded, so the two young recruits found themselves assigned to the Shattered Palace to tend to the mainframe computers that were old before the two were born. Or possibly before their parents were born, reflected Brown. And he suddenly felt very old.

Continuing their patrol, the two officers soon reached the end of the corridor and a large sealed door. The entrance to the Treasure Vault, and the reason for the existence of the Shattered Palace. Both officers presented their identification to the control panel outside the sealed door, one of the few modern devices in the facility. The door clicked and buzzed to show that it was unlocked, and the officers pushed it open as they entered. The room that they entered was clean and quiet, unlike other areas within the Palace. Banks of displays lined three walls of the small room. The fourth wall was largely taken up by windows, except at the centre where an intricate series of doors led into yet another room. The sealed room was not large, and one half contained a half-dozen racks filled with sealed containers. The other half held a half-dozen of what looked like over-sized artillery shells. Two figures clad in full-body containment suits moved within.

Brown and Frontenac gazed somberly at the scene. The clad figures turned and made sketchy salutes. Both officers sharply returned the salutes, and the clad figures returned to their duties. This was the special domain of Cpl. Fleming and Pte. Landry, where their specialized training was applied.

To Frontenac, the scene reminded him of priests clad in their vestments performing arcane ceremonies at the alter of some ancient and malevolent god. He had confessed these feeling to Brown on one occasion, and was not too surprised when his superior agreed with him. How else can one feel when one is the guardian of a cache of nuclear and biological weapons?

CHAPTER ELEVEN
Into The Maelestrom

At first Yancey thought that the noise from the banging was inside his head, the leftover byproduct of a strange dream. He'd been having a lot of those these past few days, when he slept at all. The persistence and tenor of the noise slowly made him realize that dream-time was over, and the real world was intruding into his life once again. The banging paused briefly then started up again.

With a start, his awareness clicked on and his jumped to his feet. "Office," he thought, "I'm at the office. Oh, and someone is banging on the door. Why are they banging on my door?"

Yancey was not a morning person, especially when he hadn't slept in over 50 hours. He stumbled around until he found the doorway into the front foyer, only bouncing off the door frame once. He was oddly pleased with that. Alternately smacking his lips and making "plugh" sounds with his tongue, he approached the outside door and stopped. The door was the usual kind found in business plazas, clear glass with a solid frame criss-crossing it. He peered through the door and saw his friend Simon. "What the hell are you doing here?" he yelled.

"Let me in," Simon yelled back.

"What's the secret password?" Yancey sleepily demanded.

"Oh, for fuck's sake just open the damn door. I'm bloody freezing out here!" Simon yelled back.

"Close enough," Yancey muttered as he fumbled at the lock. After a few false tries he got it open and his oldest friend stomped into the foyer, shaking the snow off his shoes. Simon opened his mouth to yell at his friend, but took one look at Yancey's bleary-eyed expression and closed his mouth. "You've been up all night, haven't you?" he accused.

"Uhm, well technically, no," Yancey said with an embarrassed note to his voice.

Simon had had to go through this with Yancey before, "OK, so how many nights *have* you been up for?"

"Two?" Yancey said questioningly, "I think. I got busy."

Simon had seen what happened when Yancey 'got busy'. Normally a pretty self-indulgent sort, when his friend got his 'detective senses' tingling his world quickly narrowed down to focus on the problem. And under that sort of intense effort problems tended to disappear, in Simon's experience. At least Simon had seen this before and knew how to help his friend deal with it. He strode towards the coffee maker only to find a caked film on the bottom of the carafe. This surprised Simon, since only the most intransigent of problems caused his friend to forget the coffee. He grabbed the carafe and took it over to the small sink to wash it out. Leaving that to drip on the counter, he turned and looked at his friend, who was still standing sleepily in the centre of the room. He'd obviously been up far, far too long. Simon guided Yancey to a chair, and sat him down. Going over to his pack, he dug inside and pulled out an energy bar. Yancey had taught him that trick, and now Simon never went anywhere without a few of them. Quickly stripping the wrapper off, he shoved it into Yancey's hands and raised it to his mouth.

"Eat," he commanded, pausing only long enough to ensure that his friend was obeying. Then he walked over to the small kitchen area and rummaged around. With no time to waste making the best coffee, Simon simply grabbed the small French press and started the hot water boiling, then quickly ground up some of the coffee beans he found in a sealed jar. Within a couple of minutes he'd made the coffee and thrust a steaming mug into Yancey's hands.

The energy bar had gotten Yancey's attention, and the hot coffee continued the job. The silence was broken only by the loud slurping of hot coffee. Then a belch. Then Yancey finally raised his head and said "This is really shitty coffee, you know. But thanks."

Simon just rolled his eyes. "Just drink it. Maybe you'll wake up enough to sleep for a few hours."

"Sleep is for the weak!" Yancey yelled in his best Klingon voice, then blearily added, "But it is starting to sound pretty good. I kinda lost track of time, I guess."

Then he sprang to his feet, almost spilling his coffee, "Wait! You're here! How'd you do that? I just got your email yesterday!" his words starting running together in his excitement.

"Settle down, hosehead," Simon replied, "That was THREE days ago. And I *told* you that I was coming up."

"Uhm. Uhm. Yeah. But. Wait, wait. Yesterday ... " Yancey stammered.

"No, three days ago," Simon patiently explained. Yancey was one of the most brilliant people Simon knew, but he really needed to stop narrowly focusing on problems to the point of physical collapse. "You done with the coffee?"

Yancey glanced down at the mug as if it had magically teleported into his hands, then swallowed the rest of the cooling liquid.

"I need to crash for a few hours. Be a good lad and check my notes while I'm away, will you? I think I'll just stretch out on the couch in the other room for a bit."

And with that he strode over to the couch in question and flopped down heavily. Within seconds he was in a deep sleep.

Simon quietly walked over and draped a coat over his friend's shoulders. "Idiot," he thought more-or-less fondly. He'd been taking care of Yancey like this for many years, ever since they were kids. Bittersweet memories surfaced unbidden. Both of them had seen some bad times growing up. Yancey had been the one that had rescued him from the dark hole in his mind, and had helped make the good times of Simon's childhood. Both their childhoods, actually. Simon knew that he was pretty smart, but Yancey had a rare and special brilliance, not to mention the strength and fearlessness to use it. What he lacked was a crucial understanding of people. Simon had the latter, and was smart enough to understand most of what Yancey went on about. They were a good team, and had kept each other sane and balanced during the bad times. Even when they'd escaped the small town hell they'd grown up in and gone their separate ways, they still kept in constant touch. Brothers in every way that mattered, their bond had stayed strong over the years. But that didn't stop Simon from wanting to strangle his friend now and again.

Simon wandered over to the large work table that was littered with the results of Yancey's latest project. It always surprised him how such a brilliant user of computers would revert to pencil and paper techniques for a project. He had to admit, though, that the technique was effective, especially for seeing the big picture at a glance. His friend was obviously looking at the attack on Toronto. Not surprising, but what were those links doing? Simon stared at the diagrams and lines for a moment, then mindlessly took off his coat and dropped it onto the floor as he missed the back of the chair. His finger traced through the links indicated, pausing only to read the text. He picked up a couple of the spiral-bound notebooks that his friend favoured, and flicked through them quickly to get the sense of them. It was all fairly straight-forward, with neat columns of notes and references to other pages. What was odd was the recurring doodle of the number eight - that wasn't like Yancey. Then he sat down, grabbed a blank pad of paper and started making his own notes as he traced through what his friend had done. All thoughts of being tired or hungry or thirsty vanished as he lost himself in his friend's analysis. It was a lot like his own method of work, which was not surprising since the two of them had developed it for their schoolwork and other projects. Time passed as one friend was lost in thought and the other lost in sleep.

After several hours of deep sleep, Yancey awoke feeling quite a bit better. His dreams, although colourful and vivid, were already starting to fade from memory. His eyes flipped open and he sprang from the couch, a coat dropping to the floor. He absently picked it up and folded onto where he had been sleeping. He walked quietly into the foyer, and spied Simon bent over the worktable, an intense look on his face. Yancey dimly remembered his friend scolding him about his own focus on more than one occasion.

"Pot, meet kettle," he thought.

He spied a piece of crumpled paper on the counter

beside him, so he picked it up and with unerring accuracy bounced off Simon's unsuspecting head. Simon uttered a short, sharp yelp and sprang to his feet with a curse. Yancey chuckled. Some things never get old.

"You stink," muttered Simon darkly, "And so does your analysis."

"Yep" admitted Yancey cheerfully, "Not enough hard data for useful conclusions. But the patterns are interesting, you have to admit, especially for what is NOT being said."

He burrowed into the heap of diagrams and newspapers until he found the set of notes he was looking for. "Have you taken a look at this lot yet?"

Simon just shook his head.

"Everyone is talking about this 'Sword of Infinity Ascending' like it's some brand new thing," Yancey began, "But I don't think it is. New name, certainly, but its MO is pretty similar to a few previous attacks over the years, each larger than the last."

He shook the set of documents in the air then smacked it down on the table, "And the attack itself required a lot of specialized intel, of the breadth and depth that is more indicative of a nation-state's level of expertise rather than any private organization. And the timing of the attack, just before the Prime Minister's summit, and the types of targets is totally out of character for a classical terrorist organization. But none, NONE, of the mainstream media's talking heads are picking up on any of this. Almost of if there's a purposeful averting of their gaze from something or someone. Oh sure, the Internet has the usual assortment of paranoid speculations and rantings, but those are strangely muted. I see you've been looking at the linguistic analysis graphs. Well, those seem to indicate that the general tone of the discussions of the attack and attackers is not quite the same as a normal terrorist attack. Everything seems just a little off, but not enough to ring official alarm bells, but ..." Yancey's exposition petered off into silence.

Simon had great respect for his friend's hunches. Yancey had a great breadth of knowledge of all sorts of ways to tease interesting bits of information out of mountains of data. Though not a recognized expert in any single field, to Simon's mind Yancey was a true polymath, and a damn brilliant one. Simon had learned through long experience to put a lot of trust into these hunches, but he'd also learned to check if the hunch was simply part of an interesting but useless puzzle or part of something more substantial. Yancey tended to treat both with equal vigor, often responding to an intellectual challenge like a bull responds to a fluttering red cape.

"OK, so something's off," began Simon, "But does it mean anything significant? I mean, how far 'off' are we talking about?"

Yancey puffed out his cheeks.

"Not by much," he admitted, "But enough to make me wonder. And enough to convince me that information is being not only hidden, but that false information is being planted! If you look at all the news reports then there's more divergence and a few more contradictions that I'd expect to see. And one of the things that I find really strange is that all the reports talk about business being back to almost normal on The Street."

Yancey paused in his pacing to face his friend and demanded, "Tell me about that."

Simon paused for a moment. He'd seen those same reports, and they were true up to a point. But only up to a point. He explained all this to Yancey, about the layoffs, the shutting down of many of the small financial service firms, the sort of thing that wasn't mentioned much in the media. Yes, the big firms had happily taken up the slack, but. The magic word, 'but'. Loans were being arranged, yes, but at more onerous terms, or only if controlling amount of stock was transferred. Small companies about to hit the big time after discovering something big, were suddenly forced to sell a controlling interest just to stay alive, and at fire-sale prices. Yes, things were back to normal, but back to a new sort of normal.

"And one more thing, Yancey," continued Simon, "The timing. It was like a 'perfect storm' of economic activity that was going to make a huge difference to a lot of companies all poised to consummate at the same time. Then the attack came, and all of a sudden it all turned to shit. The big companies picked up the pieces for cheap, potential competitors were absorbed or destroyed ... it was like a death-blow to the economic ecosystem. If you look at the big players, everything looks not so bad, but the lower levels which keep the whole thing healthy and growing have been decimated. Oh, and one more strange thing. The 'big players' that profited from all this were almost all foreign-owned. None of the Canadian big players got the best bargains or gained a controlling interest in the best of the small players."

Yancey's eyes gleamed at the news. "OK, that's new. Anything else?"

"Yah," said Simon sadly, "The mass arrests."

"What mass arrests? Are you talking about the demonstrators?"

"Yah. And it's weird about that. From almost the beginning there were these protesters chanting support of those Sword crazies. Not that many in total, but a lot of small clusters. Not together as a crowd, but clusters of four or six that would spread out through a crowd. First the chanting, then taunts, and then throwing of stuff at windows and passers-by. Always the same script. Then the cops would come and just arrest everyone in sight as being part of the demonstration. Worse, these idiots would show up at the start of the business day, or lunch, and make it look like the office workers were demonstrating. All of us, my friends and associates, know someone who has been sucked up by these sweeps. That's not helping businesses recover, either! And, strangely enough, these 'spontaneous demonstrations' never seem to happen in front of certain businesses, or if they do the protesters vanish before the cops show up. Like you say, it's all a bit 'off'."

Yancey was quiet as he digested all this, then he finally said, "One of the first things I noticed about the protesters was that some of them had a symbol of some sort on the signs."

"Oh, you mean the number eight?" responded Simon, "No-one can figure out what that means, and the protesters aren't saying."

"That's not the number eight," Yancey said, "That's a 'lemniscate'. The symbol for infinity, but upright instead of on its side."

He paused to look at his friend expectantly.

"Yah, so?" began Simon, then he paused. "An upright infinity symbol. Uhm, moving upwards? Oh, shit!" he exclaimed "Infinity *ascending*!"

"Yes indeed, oh insightful one," Yancey said happily, clapping his hands once, "Infinity Ascending. Whose 'sword' launched the attack. Which begs the question : are those protesters, or those who hired them, part of the 'Sword of Infinity Ascending' or yet another unnamed part of an organization called 'Infinity Ascending'. Whichever is the case, this was well planned and carefully executed on a broader scale than anyone seems to suspect. Something very big is going on, and we're only seeing the surface."

Simon jerked upright. "I may have another dollop of nastiness to toss into the pot. Almost forgot - and it's the main reason for my visit."

He stood upright and pulled down his pants.

"WHOA!" yelled Yancey, "WHAT THE ...!"

He was cut off by Simon's "Oh shut up, you idiot," and closed his mouth. His eyes widened even further as Simon reached down to a large bandage covering the inside of one thigh, then ripped it off with a muffled scream and a steam of soft, but intense, cursing. He handed the bandage to Yancey, who took it with a certain degree of hesitation until he saw a data key embedded within it. Another muffled scream and soft cursing caused him to raise his eyes to see Simon pulling off a similar large bandage from the inside of the other thigh. With watering eyes he passed this one to Yancey, who saw a plastic bag with handwritten notes inside. The insides of both Simon's thighs were a nasty shade of red.

"There's some analgesic lotion in the kit above the sink," said Yancey in a somewhat numbed voice, "But you're on your own applying it."

After Simon had dealt with his minor trauma, and thankfully re-buckled his pants, he explained about his cargo and the reason for the security.

A few days before, his friend Gretchen had come to him with an odd request. She needed his help, or preferably Yancey's ("She mentioned you by name, old son") to examine the contents of the data stick. They were encrypted and she wasn't too sure of her ability to deal with them without damaging the data. "Don't look at the data" she had told Simon, "Just decrypt it and give me the plaintext data files."

Simon could see the worry and fear in his friend's face, as much as she tried to hide it. He took the data key, and the handwritten notes, and stuffed them into his pockets. That much he'd do on faith and trust, curiosity be damned. But he couldn't leave it at that. He couldn't stand by and not help protect his friend from whatever it was that frightened her so. He'd never seen her frightened before, and he didn't like it. Especially when she started to cry. Gretchen had never cried before. Not ever. So he gently tried to tease a bit more information out of her, while carefully sitting beside but not touching her. Gretchen didn't like to be touched, that's just the way she was, and Simon accepted that without questioning. So he sat with her, and his quiet concern helped calm her down. Then without warning she turned and grabbed his hands in hers, and looked intently into his eyes. "Be really really damned careful with that" she said quietly but forcibly, "One good man's died for what's on there. And my friend … mm-mm-my friend might be next. It's a big, nasty, political scandal. Sh-, uhm, my friend, came to me because it's too big and there's no-one else to turn to. We know the broad outline of what's going on, but that data key holds all the raw research. No-one knows I'm here, but I gotta go right now. We've got to keep up our daily routines, my friend and I, to prevent them from suspecting. Whomever they are!"

She released Simon's hands and leapt to her feet with anger in her eyes.

"We need answers to be able to fight back! And you and Yancey are the only ones that I can trust to help. I'm so sorry to drag you into this, but it's the sort of corruption that you've always fought against!"

She took a deep breath to steady herself, then continued

quickly as if afraid of losing her nerve, "They've gamed the electronic voting system and influenced elections. From the federal level on down. That's the short version. I'm told that the proof is in that data key. And with the proof we have a chance of fighting back."

She paused once again, and stood stiffly erect, "I'll understand if you want to back out."

"Yance, she stood there trembling with fear, but willing to fight Hell and Damnation! And she's my friend. A good friend. She's stood by me and helped me even when there was a cost to doing it. And she was right - this was very bad, and had to be stopped. So I agreed to help and she left."

Yancey sat quietly as his friend told his tale. He could tell that more was coming. Simon fidgeted for a few seconds before he continued.

"That was the night before I called you, Yance. I remembered all the 'tradecraft' stuff you've talked about over the years, so I knew how important it was to maintain a normal pattern of behavior. Especially with increased surveillance in the city! So I kept a low profile while I arranged to rent a car to drive up here - and that took longer than I expected, or I'd have been here sooner! Anyways, that took a couple of days. Then I got an email from Gretchen saying that she was going out of town for a few days and not to worry. A bit strange, but not so much given the circumstances. But here's the troubling bit. You know that she and I dealt with some pretty sensitive commercial stuff, right? Well, we'd gotten into the habit of adding a special phrase to our emails to each other, just as confirmation that it was one of us and not a spoof. We've actually caught a couple of spoofed messages over the years, so we've maintained that habit. But her email didn't contain any of our special phrases. Now, she was pretty rattled so maybe she forgot. Or was rushed. Maybe. So I carefully, *yes* I was careful, asked around but all that anyone had heard was that she had left town. No hint of anything wrong. So I came up here like I was planning to, and here we are."

"And the bandages?" inquired Yancey.

"Oh, I set that up right after Gretchen left. I remembered your telling me to be ready to move at an instant's notice when doing field work. That seemed to be the best way to hide it and keep it with me. The itching stopped after the first few hours, but man oh man is it starting to itch and ache now!"

Yancey had to smile at the last bit, but had to admire his friend's resourcefulness, and told him so. "OK, let's get to work. But first we need, and I mean NEED, some decent food to fuel us. This is going to be a long day."

CHAPTER TWELVE
Search The Forest For A Leaf

Simon was unhappy with Yancey's insistence on food at a time like this. But after getting a whiff of the plate heaped with delectable spicy food ('Only Mama's Deli makes food like mama used to make!'), his mouth began to water. Several large mouthfuls later, he had to admit that his friend was right, not that Simon had any intention of telling him that.

Yancey for his part had to smile at Simon's appetite. Knowing his friend as well as he did, he knew that the last few days of worry had probably dulled his appetite. As for himself, he happily tucked into his meal with relish. It had been a long several days of intense effort, and the next few would probably put all that to shame. His thoughts darkened, but he didn't let a trace of it show on his face. Retrieving the information on that data key was too important to fumble, so it was absolutely necessary to prepare properly beforehand. And that included the human side of things.

Simon was a bit put out that Yancey refused to talk about the matter before them during dinner, but not enough to stop eating. His interest in food had greatly diminished over the past few days, replaced with worry, and he'd forgotten how hungry he actually was. Some thirty minutes later, the pair arose and exited the deli, but to Simon's surprise Yancey wanted to take a walk around the small industrial park that contained his office. The crisp air actually felt rather nice, Simon thought, adding yet another item to his friend's list of successes that he was never going to be told about.

There were few lights about, and their breaths streamed into the night as they walked. It was even dark enough to see a few stars glistening in the night sky. The squeak and crunch of the snow beneath their feet was a delightful musical accompaniment to their meanderings. "I'd forgotten how nice it was to walk in fresh snow," Simon said, "Living in the middle of a city isn't really conducive to it."

Yancey's response was to inhale deeply and exhale with a whoosh, then added "Too many people don't take the time for this sort of thing these days. But I love it. I love it all … the snow, the cold, the … the … cleanliness of it. Like a fresh coat of temporary paint, showing us how clean things can be. It helps us to see the world with a fresh perspective."

"Of course," he added with a laugh, "It comes with a price! Shoveling it, or driving in it, can be a real pain in the ass. And speaking of pain, I think that ours is about to begin."

Their wanderings had taken them back to Yancey's office. Soon they were inside stomping their feet to get the snow off, and hanging up their coats. It was time to get to work.

Yancey led the way to the work area in the back of his office. He donned a white lab coat and handed one to Simon. "Anti-static," Yancey said, "And put these slips over your shoes."

He handed Simon a pair of pinkish transparent plastic booties that both slipped over their shoes. After taking care to carefully ground both of them with a length of wire, Yancey went to the small safe where the data stick and list of passwords was residing, removed them, then placed them onto a special anti-static mat on the desk top. He then started the process of booting up the several computers that were situated there.

"Because you say that this is potential legal evidence, we're going to do this by the book," Yancey said.

He then took a large camera from its storage bin and proceeded to slip in a memory card. As he worked he explained the procedure to Simon.

"First we'll take pictures of everything. Then I'll make some copies of the data key. Not the usual file by file copies, but a byte by byte image of the contents. That will allow us to create a digital fingerprint of the data to show that the copies and the original are absolutely identical."

With the photography completed, Yancey had put the data stick into a special reader, grabbed a brand new hard drive from his stack and inserted it into another device, and started typing commands into the computer. With a final tap at the keyboard he leaned back and said, "OK, the copying and fingerprinting has begun. This will take a while, depending on the size of the data stick. The label says two hundred and fifty-six gig, so maybe as much as thirty minutes. That's OK, though, 'cuz we've got other work to do."

And with that he dug out a couple of laptops, passed them to a bewildered Simon, and led him to a nearby work table.

"OK, lad, this is where your work area is going to be. Once the copy is completed, we'll back some more copies on hard drives and data sticks. I don't know what sort of file protection is being used, but some of the fancier encryption programs will wipe the data if the proper key isn't used. So we plan for the worst case. And then after that we're going to have to dig through the data and figure out what we've got. So set up whatever you need here. I'll go get the coffee brewing."

And with that he left Simon to arrange the laptops and other paraphernalia to his own preference. He looked around a grabbed some portable whiteboards and blank flip charts and arranged them.

Yancey came back after getting the coffee brewing and examined Simon's handiwork with approval. "You're probably wondering what sort of network connectivity I've set up," he said.

"Uhm, no," replied Simon, "I just assumed you've got a wireless hub around here somewheres."

"Not this time," Yancey said with a grin, "This needs to be a top security setup! The wireless hub is turned off and unplugged except for a few rare occasions. Everything is hardwired to the network, and now we need to run some cables to those laptops you'll be using."

As he said that he started rummaging about in the equipment cabinet and pulled out a couple of long CAT5 cables which he connected to the laptops.

Grabbing a long hooked rod, he reached up and pulled down some existing strings that Simon hadn't noticed were tucked into the acoustic ceiling tiles. Yancey grabbed the network cables and tied them to the strings so they were off the floor and just above head height.

"Protects the cables and makes it so we aren't tripping on them," Yancey grinned, "Done this a time or three over the years, I have. We'll run these cables to the router over there. Oh, and I've disabled access to the Internet for the time being. Maybe I'm being overly paranoid, but better safe than sorry."

"Hold on, Yancey," queried Simon, "Why disable Internet access? You've always bragged about your epic firewall and security measures!"

"True enough," Yancey replied easily, "Given some of the strange cases I've handled, I've had to install damn good firewalls, plus honeypots to fake out the script kiddies and most hackers. On the physical side, there's the fake servers in plain sight over there running a Tor node to look busy, with the real servers hidden safely away. Hell, even the incoming T1 line is physically hidden with a fake one in plain sight! Encrypted backups are automatically done periodically and sent both to hidden local drives as well as off site. I've even set up my own DNS server to minimize my Internet footprint. But I just don't think that is good enough for this. We may be dealing with government-level spooks, and the only way to be secure against that threat level is to simply disconnect."

The process of setting up took almost as long as it took for the data stick to copy. They had each just started sipping on some coffee when the computer trilled out a tune to signal completion. Yancey typed a few more commands, then waited as one of the printers spat out a rather large label filled with seemingly random characters.

"This is the 'fingerprint' that I was telling you about. I'll paste this special one-time label to the hard disk. It can't be removed without destroying it. That means a court can look at the fingerprint I created and then create a fingerprint from the hard drive to ensure that they are one and the same. I'll do a similar thing for the original data stick, but I'll stick that and the fingerprint label into a sealed evidence bag."

His hands were busy as he spoke, performing the

described actions. Once that was completed he grabbed some more hard drives and data sticks and proceeded to make some more copies. While waiting for those, he made a copy of the list of passwords, and put all the original and the first hard disk copy into the safe. Finally he was finished.

"OK, now we look at the contents."

With a few keystrokes he displayed the contents of the data stick, or rather of a copy. To Simon's dismay it came up as a stream of gibberish.

"Well that answers one question," said Yancey, "Whoever created this was clever enough to use full-media encryption. Good. Now hand me that list of passwords, will you?"

Simon passed the notes over, "I was looking at this, but didn't see the names of any of the encryption programs."

"Hmmm, yessss," Yancey said slowly as he gazed at the screen. A few more keystrokes converted the strings of gibberish into ordered rows and columns of numbers. "Hex dump," explained Yancey, "I'm looking for a … yes! There it is."

He pointed at a name that stood out against the grouping of numbers.

"That tells me what program was used to encrypt the disk."

He grabbed the sheet and laughed, "There it is! That first line isn't a password. The silly bugger used an abbreviation of the program's name. Okey dokey, Smokey, let's try to decrypt it. Just lemme call up the decryption program … and now we type in the password on the next line of the notes … and … hmmm, is that a four or a capital 'A' do you think?"

Both of them looked at the handwritten notes, and decided that it was probably the number four. Probably.

More or less. So Yancey typed in password, pressed the 'enter' key and leaned back. The screen flashed red, and the words 'INVALID PASSWORD' flashed in front of them. Then 'DATA DESTROYED' showed up. "Must have been a capital 'A'," smiled Yancey, "That's why we've got copies!"

Their next try successfully decrypted the disk, and they were presented with a list containing five files. Simon let out a groan, "Those don't look like proper filenames! That means they're encrypted as well, doesn't it?"

"Yep," replied his friend, "So we do this all again. OK, from the notes I can see at least five different passwords, so I assume that each one of those encrypted files has a different password. I like how this guy thinks! Does things properly."

And with that he went back to work.

After a couple hours of work, including wiping out three more copies of the data, they finally had the data files. Each of the original five files was a folder containing compressed files. Uncompressing everything yielded over five hundred Gigs of data files. Yancey made several copies of those files, and handed one hard drive to Simon. "This is your copy. How do you want to go about analysing this?"

Simon thought for moment and said, "How about we each spend a half-hour scanning it to get a feel for what's here. Then we re-group and share thoughts. We should be able to come up with a plan of attack."

Yancey agreed, and the two friends bent down to work at their respective computers.

"Coffee break time," Simon heard his friend say. He sat upright with a start. He'd gotten rather absorbed by what he'd seen, reading more deeply than he had planned to. "Yeah, OK," he grunted as he rose to his feet and stretched. "There's a metric shit-tonne of data there! What're your impressions?"

He gratefully accepted the mug that Yancey held out to him, and sipped appreciatively. "Damn, that's good coffee, Yancey!" he admitted.

"Life's too short for shitty coffee," Yancey intoned in his deepest voice.

They leaned against the chairs as they drank the coffee. "OK," started Yancey, "This is how I'm seeing it. The five folders are five different avenues of investigation. Folder One ("Not the most imaginative of names, is it?" Simon interjected with a smile) looks like corporate stuff. Folder Two looks like stuff related to the electronic voting machines. Folder Three seems to deal with federal political stuff. Folder Four looks to be a mish mash of conspiracy theory stuff - secret societies and that sort of thing. Folder Five seems to deal with a building or facility or something called 'Shattered Palace'. Something to do with weapons production or something. How does that jibe with your thinking?"

Simon rather embarrassingly admitted to only looking at the first two folders, and glancing at the third.

Yancey just grinned. He figured that would happen. Besides, he himself had spent most of his time on the first three folders and just glanced at the last two. Not that he would ever admit it.

"Alright, how's this for a plan. The folders I've looked at seem to hold raw data, without any summaries or analysis. Do you agree?"

Simon nodded.

"OK," continued Yancey, "That means analyzing the raw data somehow. Any ideas?"

"Yep," said Simon thoughtfully, "I figure that for a first cut we do some social network analysis on the data in the first three folders. That should give us an overview of who the players are, how they're connected, and who are the 'spiders in the web'. What have you got for that?"

Yancey nodded, "Sounds like a good way to start. The laptops already have the usual open source tools. Gephi is loaded, as well as R, Ruby, and Python. Oh, and all the appropriate libraries. Hopefully somewhere in that you'll find something familiar."

Simon gave a curt nod, "Not as bad as I thought. I can work with those. You really serious about no access to the Internet?"

The last was uttered somewhat plaintively.

"Yep," said Yancey sternly, "We should have all the software tools we need already, and I really want to play it safe. That encryption was of the no-fooling variety, so let's keep that sort of attitude for now."

He paused for a heartbeat and then continued "How about we both spend the next hour taking a first cut at the voting machine folder, since that seems to be the key to all this. Then we'll split up and then for an hour you take the corporate folder and I'll take the political one. I don't think the others are important at this point, do you?"

Simon nodded slowly, "Sounds like a plan. We have to start somewhere, and that sounds like our best bet. Hmm, hold on. How about if I take the corporate folder and you take the voting machine folder. Play to our strengths and save some time?"

Yancey had to agree that his friend had a good point.

Simon paused for a moment and then said in a quieter voice, "But I'm still worried about Gretchen. Is there something you can do to check on her?"

His voice had a pleading quality to it.

"Hmm, well, I can do the usual tracing stuff. See if she's left a significant digital footprint over the past couple of days," Yancey said thoughtfully. Then he grabbed a pad of paper and tossed it at Simon. "Write down everything you know about her. Full legal name, date of birth, place of birth, driver's license, credit card numbers, anything. The more I've got to work with the easier it will be. I've got some scripts that can churn away while we work."

Simon spent a few minutes writing furiously. At times he checked his smartphone for information. Then he sighed and passed the pad over to Yancey. Yancey took a look at it with surprise. There wasn't as much as he could have wanted, but there was an impressive amount of detail for such an impromptu request. He raised an eyebrow to his friend. Simon grinned with one side of his mouth, "We had to cover for each other more than once for stuff. And we'd gotten to trusting each other quite a bit. She's a good friend, Yance. Not in the romantic sense, but we went through the wars together, as it were."

"It's like looking for a single leaf in a forest," warned Yancey, "But I'll unleash the electronic hounds. They'll sniff away as we work."

"Hold on there, Yancey, I thought you didn't want us plugged into the Internet for security reasons! How come your hounds get to go on but not us?" queried Simon.

"A few reasons," replied Yancey, "First of all, *if* Gretchen has been abducted - and I'm not saying that she has - then whoever has taken her will be expecting someone to come looking. That shouldn't raise any flags. Secondly, I'll be linking via Tor, which will give us a good measure of data encryption and ability to hide our identity. It's not perfect, but pretty good, and probably within the limits tolerated by any hypothetical Bad Guys. Thirdly, checking up on stuff related to what's on that data key - if it's as dangerous as you seem to think it is - will ring alarm bells and activate a hostile response real damn fast. So we err on the side of caution. And, oh yes, take the battery out of your smartphone - those things can be tracked even with the airplane mode enabled."

Thus enlightened, Simon removed the battery from his phone and placed it off to one side. Then the two friends turned to their respective tasks. It was going to be a very long night.

CHAPTER THIRTEEN
The Prime Minister's Press Conference

The Prime Minister strode onto the prepared stage in his typical firm, quick, no-nonsense style. As was his wont, he carried no notes of any sort with him. As he stood at the lectern, he turned his gaze to the assembled reporters and cameras.

"My fellow Canadians. As I promised earlier, I stand before you to bring you up to date on the events of the recent summit. Your government is dedicated to an open and continuing dialog to keep you, the taxpayers of this great country, fully appraised of matters of national importance."

"As we are all aware, Canada has historically been a nation with a resource-based economy. From our beginnings as suppliers of fur, fish, and lumber, we have expanded to be a major exporting nation. Our farms are the breadbasket upon which many nations depend. Our oil and natural gas fuels industry in America, China, and Japan. Our forests supply lumber from which homes and cities across the world are created."

"As a mature nation, we must focus on our strengths. As part of a community of mature nations we must support the strengths of our partners, as they support ours."

"As part of my government's drive to 'Create the future by honouring the past', I am proud to announce a bold new initiative with our trading partners in America, Europe, and Asia. They have agreed to unilaterally slash quotas and duties on all Canadian raw materials exported to their countries! This is truly a major step forward for us all!"

"In support of this new agreement, my government is announcing, effective immediately, deep cuts to taxes for all resource-based companies in Canada. This will help drive new resource-based developments, and ensure a prosperous future for us all. I will now take a few questions."

The room was silent. Although no sign of it showed, the Prime Minister was pleased that he had surprised them. That meant that the security measures had succeeded and he would be in full control of this event.

But the silence lasted only a heartbeat, and then the cacophony of questions began.

"Mr. Prime Minister?" said one clear voice with an arm upraised.

"Yes, you there, ma'am," said the PM pointing at a young lady.

"Zandra Faheed of AJF News. What effect will this have on Canadian manufacturing?"

"Well, Ms. Faheed, I really don't see how this will have any effect at all. This agreement covers raw resources only."

Ms. Faheed quickly asked another question "How will this affect research and development in Canada?"

The PM beamed warmly, "Again, Ms. Faheed, it really shouldn't have any effect. As you know, the level of non-government research in this country has been falling for decades. And academic research has produced little of any real commercial benefit. In today's fast-moving world Canada was simply being left behind, so my government has been working tirelessly to find new solutions that will create new jobs for Canadians for generations to come. Sustainable jobs in sustainable industries."

A reporter for a leading business newspaper shouted out, "What about reports that tariffs for Canadian manufactured exports will be increased?"

The PM's face continued to smile, but less warmly, "That was not discussed during the meetings. I don't know where you might be getting that impression from. This new agreement quite clearly deals only with raw materials."

Another reporter shouted out, "Doesn't this relegate Canada to little more than an economic colony?"

The PM's expression grew distinctly chilly, "That is a rude and insulting comment! It insults not only every taxpayer in this great nation, but also the generous offer made by our partners and allies. I will take no more questions."

And with that he strode briskly away from the lectern and out into the hallway where he was met by his staff.

"Where did that question about increased tariffs come from?" the PM snarled, "Has there been a leak about the agenda for the upcoming free trade renegotiations? Who was that damn reporter, anyway … him and the bastard that talked about us becoming a 'colony'?"

One of his aides answered, "They're both from the newspapers, sir. Both of them cover the economic beat, so asking questions about manufacturing is pretty much what they do at every opportunity. But I'll have security check them out."

"Damn newspapers," grumbled the PM, "The electronic media have learned to play ball with us readily enough.

Or at least they did after we implemented the Internet override provisions. Isn't there some way we could do something like that about the papers?"

"We've got our deep-think teams working on that sir," said another aide, "But given the physical nature of their product, it's hard to throttle them back like we can the electronic-based media. We're looking at new tax regulations, but it's tough to come up with something that affects only them. And besides, they'd scream about 'freedom of the press'. Again."

"Their only freedom is to report what Canadians need to hear," snapped the PM, "And only elected officials should have the right to determine that! I want some action on this pretty soon. The sooner we get them working with us, the better off this country will be."

The party reached the exit, then entered their limousine and drove into the enveloping darkness of the night.

CHAPTER FOURTEEN
Down The Rabbit Hole

As furiously and efficiently as Yancey and Simon worked, the task took somewhat longer than they expected. This did not surprise them, old pros that they were in data mangling. Simon's task held more data, but had the advantage that it was easier to slurp into his analysis programs. Yancey had less data, but it needed more manual intervention. Their growling stomachs and empty coffee cups finally forced a halt to the work.

"Stretch break," declared Simon firmly.

"And food and fluids," added Yancey. "Want to go to Mama's, or grab some of the protein bars and juice that I've got here?"

"Uhm, how about the house special?" Simon said, "I hate to interrupt the flow right now. We can eat as we talk."

So after taking care of the call of nature, the two friends grabbed some nourishment and sat down in front of their computers. Spiderwebs connecting glowing spheres danced on their screens. After a minute of silent munching and sipping, Simon got up and went to one of the whiteboards.

"How about if I start?" he said, picking up a dry

marker, but only to tap into his hand. "I've got some really strange stuff. OK, Canada's business ecosystem is pretty interconnected, and always has been. This means that there's a lot of the same people on the boards of directors of public companies, and that makes certain types of patterns when looked at using social network analysis. That's all well known. Well, the data on the data key shows another type of pattern. That data has information on private as well as public companies. I know a few of those non-public companies and the data jibes with what I know, so as a first cut we can believe it. Anyways, it seems to indicate that there is a 'cadre', for lack of a better word, of companies and individuals that have links to a specific type of company. They seem to have hooks into the big nodes ... the companies and individuals that have the most connections to other companies and individuals. One way of looking at it is that they influence the influencers. There's not too many of those, and they all seem to be linked to foreign companies or organizations. Here's the list."

Simon proceeded to write down a list of fourteen names.

"Then I took a look at the political data files, and did a similar sort of analysis. Most of it is standard stuff that's been analyzed for years, but there's stuff in there that I've never seen! Assuming it is legit, there appears to be a similar cadre of people influencing the influencers!"

He proceeded to write another column of ten names. Stepping back he waved at what he'd written. "See anything interesting?"

Yancey had been watching intently. "There's a lot of commonality between the two columns," he said quietly. He got up and started pacing. "I looked at the electronic voting data and began looking at company ownerships. Not all of them are public companies, but once again our mysterious researcher managed to get information on even the private companies. Like you, I found a cadre of people with hooks into all of those suppliers. Each and every one."

Yancey grabbed a red marker and circled four of the names that Simon had written down. "Those ones plus three more that aren't on any of our lists. Yet, anyways."

"All that proves is sleazy behavior, the usual gaming of The System," Simon said, "Not sure it's actionable. And if it is, it'll just be the usual wrist slap."

"Oh, there's more," Yancey muttered darkly, "There's emails sent back and forth between that lot and others not on that list, but I'm sure will be in the network you analyzed, and probably at the 'influencer' level. Some of the names I recognize as being big in the political back room arenas. That cadre is selling their services as election fixers. No-one in the government is responsible for it, or even seemed to know about it until 'the cadre' contacted them and offered to 'help' with the last election."

"Oh shit," breathed Simon, "This keeps getting better and better, doesn't it? Crooked, self-serving political cheats is one thing. But this means that they're pretty much owned by someone else behind the scenes! And given that the federal government is mandating that these same systems be used provincially, and eventually at the municipal level ..." Simon's voice trailed off briefly, then he carried on "That means that they sell the election to the highest bidder!"

"Or else," said Yancey quietly, "They're ensuring that the people they want in power, get in and stay in power."

Both were silent for a time, and then Simon spoke up, "Hold on. There is a huge amount of data there. It'll take weeks to properly go through it all. Maybe we're seeing something that isn't really there, or misinterpreting the data."

Yancey shook his head, "I don't think we're that far off. Yes, there is a lot of data there to look at, but whoever did the original research did a pretty good job of organizing and setting it up. It's a bit rough, but tons better than basic raw data. Even so, we've identified the players, if not the details of their roles."

He strode over to his computer monitor, "See here and here. Those are the cadre members. See how they connect to those people here and here? And those people in turn talk to everyone else. No, we've identified the 'influencers of the influencers', all right."

He clicked on an icon to show another graph, "Here's how the emails flowed around to all the players. See the cadre again? Almost everything goes through them. I've not read each and every email they saw, not by a long shot, but all the ones I've sampled have been high-end stuff, not day to day trivia."

Simon's face was a study in granite. He walked over to his own computers and showed Yancey a similar series of diagrams.

"OK," said Simon, "We've found a cadre of influencers. We don't know the details, at least not enough that would stick legally. Hell, all we've got so far isn't much above the level for the conspiracy discussion groups! Speaking of which, how come this isn't already in the news? Whistle blowers are coming forward all the time, how come not for something this big? This isn't just Canadian news, this is international. Has to be. Our data is mainly for Canada, but there's enough pointing to other countries!"

Yancey was starring intently at the various diagrams, "We need to refine our analysis. Reduce or eliminate uncertainties. How about if we switch and work with each other's data? Our methods are different enough for that to be a good check."

Simon agreed and they got back to work.

A couple of hours of furious work later, they decided to take another break. They munched protein bars and sipped juice in silence for a few minutes, then Yancey got up and started talking.

"Your analysis was pretty good, Simon. Knowing what to expect saved me some time and gave me ideas on how to extend it. I ran a cluster analysis on the network - which ended up pretty much the same as yours, by the way - and ran into yet another puzzle. There appears to be at least three or four distinct cadres! And that held no matter which algorithm I used."

Simon's eyebrows went up, and Yancey strode over to his computer and clicked until a coloured network diagram showed up.

"Now watch as I run the cluster analysis."

He clattered a bit at the keyboard and then stepped back. The network on the screen seemed to writhe as the components and interconnections readjusted themselves before finally settling down. Simon moved closer to the screen and gazed intently.

"Well, damn. You're right. Write those down on the board, will you?"

"No need," replied Yancey with a grin, "If you'll move aside, I'll show you why."

He proceeded to do some more clicking with his mouse, showing firstly the original network diagram and then another.

"See the second one? That's the political side. Notice anything … interesting?"

"The cadres are the same. It's the same damn groups with their fingers into everything," muttered Simon, the colour draining from his face.

"And one of those," he pointed his finger at one cadre shown on the screen, "Has links to the vote rigging racket."

He thought furiously for a moment then sighed heavily, "OK, we've got multiple groups that seem to control various aspects of Canadian business and politics. The questions to ask at this point are what does this control mean, and what exactly is being controlled. How about if I dive back into the economic analysis side? Maybe that'll give us a clue as to what the game these guys are playing actually is. Are they working together, or what?"

Yancey agreed with his friend, "That sounds reasonable. We have a snapshot of what is happening now, but no context. And that sort of thing is your expertise. I'll take a closer look at the other two folders, Four and Five, and see if there's anything that ties into what we've found so far."

So, back into their electronic world they went, ignoring the sun as it emerged and began to sink again. Finally they each emerged from their virtual worlds into the real one.

Simon spoke urgently, "Dibs on the bathroom!" as he dashed towards the facility. This led Yancey to reflect on the sometimes advantages of working alone. Finally Simon emerged and Yancey did the dash-dance into the facilities, happily emerging a couple minutes later.

"OK, why don't you go first," said Yancey, the smile leaving his face. If Simon had been more alert, he would have been worried about his friend's sudden change of mood. But as it was, he got up and walked over to one of the flip boards and started writing.

"It looks bad, Yance, real bad. The cadres control all the major industrial groups in Canada, from raw resources to manufacturing to utilities. They do this by controlling the big players and the best of the middlin' players. I added some historical financial data that I had on the laptop I brought with me to get an idea of how this control might vary over time. I'll need access to the Internet to get some better data, but even with what I've got the picture is pretty clear. The cadre have not only been controlling the major industrial groups, their control has been pretty constant over time, at least as far back as the 1940's, which is as far back as my data goes. What *has* changed is what each of the cadres controls. It looks like fights for control! Major shifts in which cadre controls what appears to occur relatively suddenly at specific points in time, rather than gradually. For example, there was a large shift just after the tank attack a few days ago. And another in the 2007-2011 time frame, just before and during the depression. A similar pattern follows for every recession or depression or major world conflict. Notice that I said 'just before' every time. That scares me, quite a bit. It either means that someone has knowledge of what was to come, or arranged for the events in question. They're using our economy, and economy of other nations, as the battlefield for their struggles! The difference with this latest round of control fights is that it's changed our economy. Remember how I described our financial setup as an ecosystem? Think of, say, a lake filled with fish. There's all sorts of fish ranging in size. Lots of little one, somewhat fewer middle-sized ones preying on those, and a few big ones that rule it all. Well, after the tank attack and the frenzy of financial dealings, the middle-sized ones are all but gone, as well as a lot of the small ones."

Yancey just looked blankly at Simon.

Simon sighed, and began to try a different tack.

"The little fish are the small one or two or three person shops. That's where a lot of new kids get their start, or the mavericks try out new ideas. It's both a training ground and a breeding ground for innovation. It's how a lot of new companies start out. Many fail, but a few blossom into something larger. That's where the medium-sized companies come in. They're the small ones that get bigger. That's where the new ideas really start to take off, because now these companies have the resources to finally make things happen in a very real way, rather than just dreams and promises. At this point they either grow into a big fish or get eaten - I mean grow large or get taken over. It's an ecosystem, with constant churn to keep things healthy. Well, more or less. Anyways, after the last crisis caused by the tank attack, a lot of the medium and small companies got absorbed or made bankrupt. More importantly, those tended to be the ones that were the innovators. Maybe the next Blackberry or Nortel. Except that now they'll never be able to grow. They're extinct or bought up. The loss of the small ones means a loss of training grounds for the new kids, like myself. The loss of the medium ones means no place for us to go. A whole lot of expertise is going wasted with no where to go except out of the country or to work for the few remaining big fish. And all of the important players, in all the important industries, are controlled by the cadres. Who are all foreign. And amoung the cadres, there's been a real shakeup. Historically there were as many as a dozen of them. The ones that we discovered in the data stick are the survivors that existed up to the time of the tank attack. At least one of those has been eliminated since. There's only two, maybe three, cadres left."

Simon fell silent, drained both by the strain of the sustained effort and the knowledge that he'd uncovered.

Yancey said quietly, "I'm afraid that I can only add more depth to that cesspool. I've been looking at Folder

Four, what we called a 'mish mash' of stuff. It is that, but only because of what it is trying to uncover. Its got stuff on a number of 'secret societies' like the Bilderbergs, Skull and Bones, and several others, some of whom I've never heard of. And you know how I enjoy a good conspiracy theory!"

Both men smiled at that. Some people like to read murder mysteries, but Yancey Franklin loved to read about conspiracies. It was always fun to try and unravel the logical fallacies, circular references, and sometimes bat shit crazy nonsense. Still, many of them started with an observation of something real. Maybe misinterpreted or misunderstood or a minor event taken out of context, but real enough.

"If I'm reading the material correctly, and I think I am, the original researcher had found a number of leads regarding these secret groups. There are even some companies mentioned specifically, and those are in the cadres we've found. The evidence also points to conflicts between these groups, spanning decades. At least to the early 1900's, if not earlier. It even mentions one group, almost in passing because there is little known about it. It has links to some, but not all, of the other secret groups. It's called 'Infinity Ascending'."

Simon could only gawk at his friend, and stand there blinking in confusion.

Yancey continued, "The few mentions of Infinity Ascending associate it with events, both major and minor, that result in one cadre triumphing over another in some way. Internationally."

Simon shook his head as if to clear it, "No, wait ... wait. It's sheer lunacy to blame every bad thing on some evil group or other. You know that, and better than anyone!"

Yancey had to agree but pointed out that their own

research showed that local power groups either submitted or were destroyed. At least in an economic sense.

"We'd have to do a more thorough historical search regarding the individuals involved to see if anything more 'personal' was done," he pointed out. Then he yawned mightily, which caused Simon to follow suit.

"Look, Simon, we're dead on our feet. Brains nearly mush. We've got to get a few hours sleep. All this is ... overwhelming, to say the least. You sack out on that sofa over there and I'll grab the big comfy chair over there."

Simon began to protest that there was still too much to do, but pretty quickly realized that his friend was right. They were both shambling zombies, and liable to make mistakes if they kept going. So he went over to the offered sofa and stretched out, yawned, and fell asleep almost at once.

Yancey smiled at his friend, grabbed a blanket and covered him with it. Then he straighted up and his eyes were brighter than they were a moment before. He had a lot more experience at pushing himself during an investigation than Simon, and there was work to be done. He'd just begun looking at the contents of Folder Five, and given what they'd already learned he was beginning to get a bad feeling. For starters, where had a newspaper reporter gotten his hands on this stuff? For another, the timestamps on Folder Five indicated that it was created shortly before the death of the reporter. Yancey was afraid that he and Simon had fallen down a rabbit hole to Hell, and the only chance of survival was to learn as much as possible as quickly as possible.

CHAPTER FIFTEEN
Road Trip

Simon was in a warm, comfortable, happy place. Life was easy, life was good. Suddenly everything went cold and wet. He awoke spluttering with a cold, wet washcloth laying over his face. He sprang to his feet uttering a shrill, "Glagh!"

His eyes squinted at the brightness of the lights in the room, and for a moment he stood there trying to figure out where he was, and why he was there. A large, sort-of-soft bundle hit him in the midsection and he fell back to the couch with a heartfelt, "oof."

"Wakey, wakey sunshine!" exclaimed a rather too energetic Yancey, "We're bugging out and hitting the road!"

Simon could only repeat his "Glagh?" but in a steadier, more interrogative tone.

"Indeed, my lad, indeed!" his friend replied, "Now how about hauling that bag out front?"

Simon looked down at the duffel bag in his lap, and got unsteadily to his feet. He had never been an easy riser. He shuffled with his burden to the front office and dropped it down beside the other bags he saw there. Slow to wake up he might have been, but he was rapidly coming to his senses.

"OK, what gives?" he demanded of Yancey, who had walked up carrying a large plastic storage container.

"Road trip," was the terse reply.

Simon was now fully awake and becoming rather peeved. He opened his mouth to blast his friend, but Yancey began talking quickly.

"I stayed up to do a bit more reading while you slept. We've got to get out of here. Several reasons. Reason one is that we're too exposed here. Reason two is that the bad guys are way badder than we thought. Reason three is Gretchen."

At the mention of his friend's name, Simon grew quiet, "So what did you find about her?"

Yancey hadn't stopped arranging the boxes and bags he was piling up.

"Nothing definitive, but nothing bad," he assured his friend, "But we gotta go. I've got the Busted Flush out front. Let's start loading it up."

And with that he picked up a couple of duffel bags and headed outside to the car. Simon grabbed a couple more and followed him. He trusted Yancey's judgment implicitly, and knew that answers would be forthcoming as soon as the immediate concerns had been taken care of.

The trunk of the 2007 Crown Victoria, of the Police Interceptor variety, was open. Its cavernous interior accepted the bags without crowding. Another couple of trips managed to fill it up, plus much of the back seat. Included in the equipment were a couple of empty coolers, blankets, coats, boots, and knapsacks.

"Jeez, Yance, do ya think we're taking enough stuff?" Simon said somewhat sarcastically.

"Not enough, actually," Yancey admitted, not taking any offense at his friend's tone, "We need to continue our research, just not here. Not sure where, but I'm thinking that a campsite off the beaten track might not be a bad idea. I've got proper camping stuff back at my apartment. We'll swing back there and grab sleeping bags and a tent. Oh, and some more clothes would be a good idea. I've packed what I had here at the office, and that'll do the both of us for a few days. But more would be better. Especially something for cold weather."

Yancey paused to survey the results of their loading and nodded, "Not the optimum packing job, but good enough for now. Let's go inside, hit the washroom, then grab the last minute stuff and go."

With that he shut all the doors to the car and went back inside, followed by Simon.

Taking care of nature's call only took a few minutes. Yancey boiled up some water and put that into an insulated container. Then he filled up a few more large containers with tap water. Taking a modest sized duffel bag, he walked around and grabbed all the portable foodstuffs he could find, which wasn't too much since they'd been dipping into the larder pretty heavily over the past couple of days. Not to worry, he thought, there's plenty more at the apartment. One last look around, and they were about ready to leave.

Simon suddenly jerked erect and exclaimed, "What about the laptops?"

Yancey replied, "Already packed in a duffel that we put into the back seat. Printouts of all the analysis we did are packed as well. And a couple of large fully-charged UPS's for backup power. Oh, slip this stuff onto your belt."

He handed a couple of small belt pouches to Simon.

"One contains data sticks with copies of the raw data and our analysis. The other has a survival kit." He paused for a moment then handed over a long, leather-encased object, "This is a combat knife. It goes onto the back of the belt, at the small of your back."

He showed Simon the same item on his belt, along with similar pouches. "It's not too large, won't interfere with sitting, and won't fall out of the sheath. Hopefully we'll never have to use it. But better safe than sorry."

Simon undid his belt and loaded it up as instructed, without comment. Yancey took security seriously, and it did make sense. With that done they packed up the remaining gear and headed out to the car, loading it onto the floor of the rear seat.

Just then, 'Mama' strolled up, "Greetins', boys. Where ya'll off to in sech a hur-ray?"

His broad, warm Jamaican accent seemed to add extra weight to his inquiry.

Yancey smiled broadly and said heartily, "Road trip! We haven't been on one in ages, and with Simon laid off and me between jobs, well, no time like the present, eh?"

Mama wasn't fooled. He'd known Yancey too long, and was too keen an observer of life, "An' you goin' witout any o' my cookin'! Na, na, boys, ya gotta take something for th' road. Folla me."

And with that he turned and walked to his deli. The 'boys' looked at each other, then Yancey shrugged, and they both followed Mama. As much out of curiosity as hunger, despite Yancey's urgency to be gone.

Stepping into the deli made their mouths water and their stomachs rumble in protest at their emptiness and mediocrity of the food over the past couple of days. Mama started scooping various foods into containers and putting them aside in silence. "Yancey, if the problem is your rent money ... I can speak to the landlord," he began slowly, knowing that although Yancey was a good detective he was a lousy businessman. In fact, Yancey had helped him

99

out on more than one occasion for small but important matters, shrugging off offers of payment.

Yancey was embarrassed into silence by Mama's offer. Finally he said, "No, no, nothing like that. Rent's paid up for the next month. Just gotta hit the road."

Mama just quietly stared at Yancey while ladling food into containers.

Yancey sighed. This was not going to be easy.

"Remember Simon's friend Gretchen? She was up here with Simon a couple or three years ago? Well, she's run into some trouble in Montreal and we're going to try and help."

Mama glanced at Simon, whose face showed the essential truthfullness of that statement. Mama sighed and said, "Simon, you a good boy. Ya keep Yancey here grounded. An' Gretchen seemed like a good girl. But, boy, she ain't the one for you."

Surprisingly Mama was getting embarrassed, the first time Yancey had seen that happen. Equally surprising, at least to Yancey, was that Simon just laughed. Yancey turned and stared at his friend.

"Mama, I know she's a lesbian," chuckled Simon, "And things aren't 'that way' between us. Never were, never will."

Then he became more serious, "But I think she might be in trouble. She's my friend, and she's always been there for me."

Simon fell silent.

Mama had stopped his work in embarrassment, but started up again. This time filling up plastic bags with pastries, breads, and buns.

"You got a cooler for this stuff?" was all that he said.

"I'll go back to the car and get them," said Simon, as he turned and trotted out the door.

Mama turned to Yancey, his eyes showing sorrow in their depths, "It be more than that, Yancey boy," he said simply.

"Mama ..." Yancey began.

"Never mind. What did you plan to do about Simon's car? It'll be a rental I'm thinkin'."

"Oh, hell, I forgot about that!" exclaimed Yancey with some shame.

"Never be mindin' that. Give me the keys and I take care of it. Do you want it returned or disappeared?"

Yancey was taken aback only briefly, then he thought for a moment, "Returned. That makes the most sense."

His voice was tight and professional. Mama's mood lightened. He'd seen Yancey in 'detective mode' more than once, and was satisfied that the young man was fully 'in the game'.

"Oh, and if anybody asks about us, don't hold back any information. Nothing at all. Tell the complete truth," he said looking intently at Mama. Mama just nodded, but he was beginning to worry about what the younger man had gotten himself into *this* time. He kept stepping into places where he shouldn't, private detective or no. What he needed was to meet a nice girl to settle him down. Mama sighed silently. Kids these days were just too full of their own lives to settle down and appreciate life. Although, he had to admit, at that age he'd been equally hellbent on adventures. But still. His thoughts were interrupted as Simon came banging through the door carrying two plastic coolers.

Mama began to quickly and efficiently fill them, waving away any help from the young men, "Did either of you think to make any ice or cooling packs?" he asked, knowing full well that the answer would be negative. Without pausing for an answer he grabbed some cooling packs from his fridge, and put them into the cooler that held the perishables, "OK, this cooler be holdin' hot stuff. Eat these first. Should be good for a couple of days at least if you keep 'em cold after they cool down."

He pointed at the other cooler, "This one be holdin' salads and bakery goods and cold meats. After the cool packs are done, eat the meats quick."

He was interrupted by the slamming of his back door. Everyone started, and Mama's hand edged towards a large knife that was laying on the counter. Mama's wife seemed to materialize in front of them, she was moving so quickly.

"Yancey!," she exclaimed, "You be safe!"

Then she ran around the counter to embrace the embarrassed young man, then just as quickly stepped back while shaking his shoulders, "Don' be scarin' an old woman that way!"

The puzzled looks on all their faces made her realize that no-one had any idea of what she was talking about.

"Your apartment, Yancey - it be on fire! Just heard about it on th' news as I be drivin' over!"

Yancey simply turned to Mama and said urgently, "We have to go," and carefully but kindly removed the hands on his shoulders.

Mama came from behind the counter carrying one of the coolers, which he handed to Simon. He then went and got the other cooler and handed it to Yancey. "Go," was all he said, to his wife's puzzlement. A look from him promised details later, so she knew that this was not a time to interfere.

Yancey turned to go, then stopped and said to Simon, "Give Mama the keys to your car. He'll take care of it."

Simon looked startled, but complied after putting the cooler on the floor. Then he picked it back up and the two young men quickly marched out to the Busted Flush. As they went Simon turned to wave, nearly dropping the cooler. Yancey just turned and gave a big grin then kept going. The game was afoot!

Mama and his wife waved at the departing adventurers until they drove off. His wife turned to Mama and stated, with some emphasis, "Now would be a FINE time for explanations, you."

Mama sighed. His wife was unhappy with Yancey's adventuring ways, and this was not going to ease her mind. In truth, though, his own mind was far from easy about his young friend.

The Busted Flush drove down the highway towards Montreal, purring happily. Its 250 horsepower V8 engine had no problem with the car's weight nor the extra weight of the passengers and luggage. This was a car built for hard use.

"When, exactly, did you have time to do all this extra investigating? We were supposed to be resting," Simon said accusingly.

"It was only a little bit of extra reading. And then I slept. A bit. Honest."

Yancey could feel his friend's eyes boring into him.

"No, really! I did get some sleep! Word of honour!"

Simon just grunted and was silent for a bit. He knew full well that could mean as little as a five minute nap. But he let that go, for now. Something had Yancey spooked.

"So?" was all he finally said.

Yancey sighed, "My basic checks on Gretchen didn't turn up too much. I found out some stuff that you neglected to tell me, like she was born and raised in Montreal until she completed one year of CGEP, then she moved to Thunder Bay for college for a couple years, then she transferred to the University of Toronto where she got a Masters in business studies. Her driving record is clean except for one speeding ticket that she got when she was seventeen. She has little Internet presence, with no Facebook page, and a Twitter account that she uses sparingly. No debts that I can see, no criminal record, just a plain and simple life."

Yancey paused for a few seconds. "So I dug a bit deeper, and looked at her credit card history."

Simon was startled at that, "I thought those were only available with a warrant or official police request at the very least."

"Uhm. Well. Yeah," Yancey said hesitantly, "But I know someone who owes me a favour and they kind of, well, hacked into the records for me."

He saw the look on his friend's face and hurriedly went on, "And no, I don't like to do this, but this was an emergency."

Simon sighed, but nodded his agreement, "So, what did you find with your illegal search?"

"Nothing unusual," Yancey replied, then paused before adding "Mostly."

Simon waited more or less patiently for Yancey to go on. After a few seconds Yancey continued with a sigh, "The records show her renting a car in Toronto, and arranging to drop it off in Montreal as a one-way trip. She apparently bought gas at a roadside gas bar off Highway 401 in Oshawa, then got gas in Montreal, then got a motel room in Montreal for one night, then no more charges."

Simon thought a moment and said, "Well that's pretty straight forward, isn't it? She must be in Montreal staying with relatives."

Yancey didn't answer for a moment, then quietly asked, "How come she didn't get gas anywhere between Toronto and Montreal? That's over 560 km from one gassing up to the next. Even for a compact car, that's a long way to go without getting any gas. Possible, but she'd be running awfully low. Gretchen didn't strike me as the sort that would push things to the limit like that. Is she?"

Simon slowly shook his head, "No. She didn't own a car, but would rent one on the rare occasions she needed one. Hell, she wouldn't even let it get down to half full, even if it was someone else's car and they were driving. Kinda fussy that way."

He paused for a moment then continued, "But maybe she paid with cash? You know, if she though someone was after her and she didn't want to give her location away by using her credit card?"

"Good point," said Yancey, "But she'd already broadcast her destination as being Montreal. And used her credit card in Toronto and Montreal. No, it smells. Too easy, too pat. I've tracked enough people to get a feel for this sort of thing. This looks OK on the surface, but that's all. Like it was planted. Maybe 'they' were rushed or got sloppy. I'm pretty sure that it's all designed to make it plausible to assume that she's in Montreal."

He paused, then added, "I can't find any trace of her other than that. That could be good or bad. I really can't know one way or the other."

"So explain to me, oh Master Detective, why we are heading to Montreal?" inquired Simon politely, if a bit testily.

"To lay a plausible trail of our own. Speaking of which, let's pull off here to fill up on gas."

And with that Yancey pulled off the highway into a roadside gas bar. There he filled up, then went inside to pay the cashier with his credit card. While there he chatted with the cashier, bought a few chocolate bars, and inquired about the best route to Montreal. The cashier grabbed a map, showed Yancey the route and mentioned the roads to avoid because of construction. Yancey thanked him, and purchased the map. Then he walked back to the car and pulled back onto the highway.

He half-expected Simon to be seething with impatience, but instead Simon simply looked thoughtful. After a few minutes of silence Simon asked, "So what else did you find in the files? Something spooked you, and it wasn't the news about Gretchen. We're making everyone think that we're off to Montreal, so obviously that's not the plan. So again, what's got you spooked, and what's the plan?"

Yancey was impressed by his friend's analysis, and said so. Then he paused for a heartbeat and explained, "In reverse order of your questions, we're going to Thunder Bay. We'll head along here for a while, then cut over to the Quebec side of the river and double back. As for why Thunder Bay, that's what's got me scared. The why of it is going to take a bit of explaining."

Yancy paused for a moment then continued, "Remember Folder Five, the one with something or other called 'Shattered Palace'?"

Simon nodded.

"I found out what it is. It's a very secret military installation used to store nuclear warheads, as well as chemical and biological weapons. And the Sword of Infinity Ascending is going to be attacking it sometime in the next week."

The car was silent for a time.

Then Simon exploded, "ARE YOU OUT OF YOUR FUCKING MIND!"

After a few seconds of incoherent sounds he finally settled down and said in a quieter, but still strained voice, "Canada doesn't have any nuclear weapons. We got rid of all of them decades ago. *And* the chemical shit *and* the germ shit."

He was breathing heavily now, "Oh, please God, tell me that you're wrong about this!"

Yancey knew that his friend was vehemently opposed to weapons of mass destruction, but had never seen him get this upset when discussing it.

"Uhm, well," Yancey began, "It looks real enough. And the Sword thinks so, too. There's diagrams of the base layout, personnel lists, shift schedules, and even vacation schedules. There's gaps, at least in the stuff our original researcher had, but enough to indicate a severe leak of a lot of sensitive information. This looks like a real place, Simon! And the Sword plans on hitting it, just like they hit Toronto! It's just a preliminary battle plan, but it talks about required troop strengths and weapons. Speaking of weapons, it looks like they plan to use some sort of advanced body armour and weapons, along the lines of the US Army's 'Future Soldier' program, only more advanced. Did you ever hear about that?"

Simon nodded, "Yeah, I saw something about that on Discovery Channel. Didn't it get canceled a few years ago or something?"

Yancey nodded, "Yep, but a lot of those big-ticket research things never really die. They just change the names. Especially if a favoured weapons supplier is involved."

"OK," said Simon, "Explain to me about the nukes and shit."

Yancey focused on driving for a minute then said, "We'll be turning off in a few minutes. How about I hold off on that until we get turned around? These interchanges and local roads get funky."

Simon agreed with a smile. He'd gotten lost on these things more than once.

Ten minutes later the two found themselves on the Quebec side of the Ottawa River heading west. Yancey took up his tale.

"The files don't go too much into the history of it all, but we can take a pretty good guess. It's way before our time, but the history of the Cold War era has always been a fascination for me. In the late 1950's, John Diefenbaker was leader of the Conservative Party and head of the government. The Americans were putting a lot of pressure on him to agree to put missiles on Canadian soil to counter the perceived Soviet threat. Dief was a staunch nationalist and feared losing control to the Yanks. So he waffled and finally agreed to install a missile system called 'Bomarc' to appease them. However, to appease Canadians he declined to arm them with the nuclear warheads that they were designed to carry. This pissed off the Yanks, to say the least. However, the opposition Liberal Party, led by Nobel peace prize winner Lester Pearson, firmly supported the use of nuclear weapons in Canada. In 1963 a group of cabinet minsters claimed that Dief had lost the confidence of not only them but the entire country as well, over this and other issues. A short time later a mid-term election was forced, and the Liberals became the government. Later that year the Bomarc missiles were armed with nuclear warheads. This was followed by nuclear armed tactical missiles being issued to Canadian NATO forces in Germany. Then nuclear armed air-to-air missiles for continental defense in Canada and in Europe."

Yancey paused.

"But we haven't had any nukes for decades!" exclaimed Simon.

"Yes, exactly," noted Yancey, "The Bomarc was phased out in the early 1970's, as were the tactical nuclear missiles in Europe. Then the tactical nukes on aircraft missiles were slowly phased out. But it was only in the 1980's when we got the CF18 fighters to replace the CF100's and CF104's that all the missiles using nuke warheads were phased out. The CF18 used missiles with conventional explosives, but they were far superior in range and accuracy than the missiles armed with nukes ever were. And so ended the era of nuke warheads in Canada. More or less. We didn't have any permanently stationed here, but that didn't stop the American ships or planes carrying nuke warheads from cruising around and making stopovers."

Yancey paused briefly as he navigated some curves in the road before continuing.

"Anyways, the Sword seem to think that there are still some stored at the Shattered Palace facility, whatever that is. About a dozen of them. From the description they seem to be of the type that were called 'tactical' weapons, with a yield of one to three kilotons. Small, portable, and very destructive for their size. There is some indication that there might be two or three somewhat larger ones, but nothing of the city-killing sizes. These are strictly for battlefield use. Any questions so far?"

Simon just numbly shook his head, his widened eyes revealing his shock.

Yancey fully understood his friend's confusion and horror. He'd had the same reaction, but had more time to adjust to it. He simply said, "There's a roadside stop up ahead. How about if we pull over and have some coffee and food? We need to be careful to stay on top of our own needs, right now."

Simon nodded his agreement, so a minute later found them pulled over into a deserted rest stop. There was a bit of snow covering the picnic table, but they quickly took care of that. They put a tarp over the plank seat to keep dry. Sipping gratefully on the coffee supplied by Mama, they slowly started eating some of the stew. Becoming aware of how hungry they were, they quickly focused their attention on the stew, then on the soft chewy buns. Sighing happily, they leaned back facing outwards with their backs against the table. The chirps of small birds echoed in the stillness. The sun even deigned to come out and brighten up the world.

"So," said Simon eventually breaking the comfortable silence, but not wanting to sully the glory of the day with the horrors they'd been learning about.

"So," agreed Yancey.

And the silence continued.

"Why are you still driving that damn land yacht of a car?" Simon finally asked with honest wonder, "It's not exactly inconspicuous. Not the sort of thing a PI should be driving, I would have thought."

"Hey! Don't go dissin' my ride, bucko! This car is a classic!" Yancey shot back.

"Hmm," muttered Simon, "I can still remember you working that last summer in town for that plumbing outfit. On call day and night. Loads of overtime. That was your college money! And instead you blew in all on this car. How did you ever convince the police chief to sell it to you, anyways?"

Yancey smiled with the memory of it, "Good times, good times," he murmured, knowing even as he said it that his mind was filtering out the bad stuff. But that was OK. It was his and Simon's last summer in that small town. The last time either of them ever stepped foot in it, for that matter. For all the bad times, there were some shining good ones. That last summer had some of the best, too. A good, if some what messy, job. Money in his pocket for the first time, or at least money that he was able to keep. As for the chief, well, he'd been able to help out with a case in a small way. But enough that the chief let him buy one of the used Crown Victoria's that the force was phasing out. A good one, too. And having discovered the joys of the 'Travis Magee' novels that summer, he named it 'The Busted Flush' after the houseboat of the fictional detective, not to mention in honour of the job that allowed him to purchase it. A good car, able to give out and accept physical punishment. Reliable, repairable, and built like a tank. He loved that car. But all he said to Simon was, "It's a damn good car, and it's never failed me. Never."

Simon understood what was left unspoken. He had his own bittersweet memories of that last summer, too.

Yancey cleared his throat, "That reminds me, I gotta do something. Grab the dishes."

He grabbed the cooler and walked back to the Busted Flush. Simon followed carrying dishes and bits-and-pieces. Yancey pulled open the rear door, rummaged about for a bit and pulled out a plastic bag, thrusting it at Simon.

"Put all the garbage into this, and we'll toss it into the waste bin over there."

He continued rummaging as Simon obligingly took care of the garbage. As he returned, he saw Yancey under the Busted Flush, pulling and pushing at various points.

"Look, I know you love your car and all. Should I be leaving you two alone for a while?" was all he said, smiling.

"Oh shut up," Yancey retorted. He rolled out from under the car and started brushing the snow and dirt from his cloths and hands. "Pass me that jug with hot water we packed, will you?" he asked. Simon obliged by taking the container and pouring it over Yancey's hands as the latter scrubbed the last of the crud off. Simon re-capped the jug and put it back into the car.

"Going to tell me what that was all about?" he asked.

Yancy grinned, "Insurance. I slipped some spare data sticks into hidey-spots under the chassis. A couple of them are clever but obvious, so they're meant to be found by any half-competent searcher. But there's a couple spots that are real buggers to find. Like I said, insurance."

Simon looked puzzled.

Yancey laughed, "There's nothing visual to show up in a search. Well, now there's some smudged areas but those'll be gone in seconds after we start driving. What the pros use is an electronic detector. Sort of like a metal detector, in fact. It sends out special radio signals that react with any electronics, including data sticks. Those special hidey spots that I mentioned are embedded behind where the car's electronics and power cables run. That's probably how our original data stick got overlooked. Didn't you say it was hidden in a power socket?"

Simon nodded.

"So I think we're good to go," said Yancey, "Let's hit the facilities for a quick bio-break and then we're off."

A couple of minutes later saw them leaving the site. As they hit the road, Yancey stopped the car and got out. Grabbing a branch that he'd spied, he smudged the tracks that they'd left in the snow. He couldn't do anything about the picnic table but that could be explained by animal activity, so it was probably OK. Then taking care to eliminate his own new tracks, he went back to the car and hopped in, and off they roared westward.

Almost as soon as they were moving, Simon was urging Yancey to provide more details about the Shattered Palace.

Yancey was silent for a moment as he collected his

thoughts.

"We know that Canada had nuclear devices based here at home and in Europe for almost thirty years. All those warheads came from the States, and they always kept pretty tight control over them. Wherever they were housed, the Yanks kept a military unit of their own to guard them. Proper security means that the number of storage locations would be minimized, especially when exporting to foreign countries. That would be us, in this case. I can hypothesize a small number of staging areas from which the warheads would be sent out to the appropriate Canadian Forces bases. Or maybe the facility was already in use as a place to store Canada's chemical and biological weapons."

Simon interrupted him at this point with a shocked, "Canada's WHAT? I knew that we had a couple of research facilities for that shit, but I've never heard about it being turned into actual munitions!"

Yancey just nodded, "Of course there would be munitions. Can't develop proper safety equipment if you don't know, and test against, the weapons you expect to face, can you? Oh, I'm sure that it was all very properly and carefully done. But there would certainly be chemical and biological weapons made, at least of some sort. And once our country had officially pledged that we didn't have any, there would be no way to reveal them without one hellacious PR disaster. If not a full-blown international debacle. So any munitions would have to be put somewhere off the official maps. Maybe that's how this Shattered Palace place got started, with the nuclear warheads just sort of added as a 'temporary' staging thing. And once all that crap was there, especially after its politically-safe-to-reveal date, then it probably just kept going as a simple matter of bureaucratic inertia. Out of sight, out of mind. After a decade or two, no-one would know how to deal with it properly, so it would be easier and safer just to to keep it there. It has probably become something of a career-ending posting by this time. Probably a place to dump unwanted personnel, too, I would think. From the drawings, it's not all that large a place, physically, and mostly underground. There's three external doorways, referred to as 'portals'. One main one and two minor ones. Very little in the way of modern tech, from the look of it. It was probably state-of-the-art once, but that was decades ago. Long before we were born, actually. But the outside doors themselves are bloody thick, and there are all sorts of doors on the inside. Probably to act as barriers in case of a breach. The main portal leads into the main corridor, that curves back and forth like a snake, probably as a security and safety measure. At the end is a room where the weapons are stored. It's got its own bloody big door that opens into a control room. There's a single airlock that goes into the storage area. That's a two-floored, open-concept sort of thing. Nukes and biologicals on the top floor, and the chemical weapons below those. Originally, there were supposed to be upwards of sixty personnel stationed there, but over the years that's been reduced to the thirty or so personnel currently. About half of those are American forces, and from the duty roster they handle base security. Although it's on Canadian soil, overall command is handled by an American general, with a Canadian officer assigned as his number two and liaison."

Yancey paused to cough and clear his throat. He wasn't used to talking for so long, so he asked Simon to pour him a bit of coffee. After a few sips, he felt ready to continue.

"Well, anyways, that's the Sword's target. They mean to get their hands on the nukes and biologicals. I guess that chemical weapons are dime-a-dozen for their type. Hell, any standard agricultural pesticide is a pretty good weapon when the concentrations are high enough."

The overuse of pesticides was something of a sore point for Yancey, who always grumbled when he thought about them. He shook his head guiltily and continued, "The Sword's plan, or at least the preliminary version of it we've got, indicates a three step plan. Step one is to break in and gain access to the weapons. Stage two is to remove the weapons from their storage and take them somewhere - the destination isn't indicated in the plans. Stage Three is to use explosives to damage the Shattered Palace and cause the chemical weapons to spew out into the landscape. They're counting on a two to five kilometer dead zone being created, with plumes extending outwards depending on the prevailing winds."

Yancey fell silent for a moment before continuing, "The plans talk as if they've got all the necessary pass codes and keys to open every door, including the portals. They've obviously got access to the very best military tech, certainly better than anything the soldiers guarding the place have. And they're at the top of their form, I've no doubt about that. And given that the Shattered Palace is an old, forgotten facility at the back end of nowhere, I seriously doubt that the same could be said of the defending troops. As for timing, the plans call for a window of opportunity of five days. Don't know why, but that's what it says. The window starts tomorrow."

With that, Yancey fell silent.

Simon just gaped at his friend. His mouth opened and closed several times before he could make words come out. Yancey was his oldest and dearest friend, and very much like a brother. But sometimes his ability, or maybe it was just his nature, to be so coolly analytical was just too

115

much for Simon to understand. Finally he managed to blurt out, "So you've got us doing a fucking road trip when those Sword bastards are about to unleash Hell? What the fuck, Yancey!" and he fell silent, unable to say anything more.

Yancey was silent, the very image of serenity. He knew that his talent for analytical detachment was something that Simon had problems understanding, sometimes. But Yancey had learned the hard way to develop that ability, and he had gotten very good at it.

"Simon, who exactly could we tell? Who would believe us in time? And who could we trust?" was all he said, in a quiet tone.

Simon closed his eyes, trying to enforce calm upon his churning emotions. Finally he spat out, "Fine! So what's the damn plan?"

"We go to the Shattered Palace and warn them," said Yancey quietly, "I know where it is, and we can get there in just over a day, I think. Let me pull over just up ahead and I'll show you on the map."

With that, he slowed the car and pulled over onto a wide section of the shoulder. Once stopped, he reached into an inner pocket of his coat and pulled out a map. Unfolding it, he began explaining.

"The first thing is to get to Thunder Bay. The facility is north and west of there, buried in the forest and countless lakes that dot the country there. From what I can see, from Thunder Bay we take Highway 11 west, then change to Highway 17. That's take us north and west. Then about here ..." Yancey jabbed at the map, "We have to go due north, more or less. The map shows a series of minor back roads crisscrossing the area, so we'll be picking our way amoung them. We can check Google maps tonight when we stop for supper to see if there's anything that goes all the way. I've got the GPS coordinates, but that's not going to help us get there. There has to be a decent road, though, but probably not marked on any map. And probably hidden from view from any of the roads that are there."

Simon looked at the map, "Uhm, Yance, I understand your thinking about warning the troops at the facility instead of anyone else, but those minor back roads have me worried. Can the Busted Flush handle those?"

He hurriedly added "No offense!"

Yancey grinned broadly, "None taken. You haven't seen what the Flush can do, is all. We've got better clearance than most cars, and better than a lot of so-called pickups."

Yancey sneered at the mention of those. He had little use for those toys aimed at the city dweller who needed an excuse to strut around looking 'manly'.

"On top of that, the shocks are rated for severe duty, so they'll handle any potholes and bumps. The tires are police-rated snow tires. And we've got a damn powerful V8 engine that is tuned properly for low-speed use. The Flush can handle anything that doesn't require a four wheel drive."

Yancey wasn't one to idolize technology, but he was very fond of his car. It had saved his life more than once.

Simon frowned as he looked at the map, "We can make better time if we take turns driving. In fact," he said with a frown, "You could probably use a break about now. I know you handle all-nighters better than me, but I'm sure that you could use a rest about now."

Yancey grunted his agreement, and added a wry lopsided smile.

Simon pressed his advantage, "There's a lot of straightforward, boring driving for the next few hours. We'll swap after we stop for supper. Uhm, how about at one of the provincial parks just east of Thunder Bay?"

Yancey looked at the map and nodded his agreement, then opened his door and got out. He stretched for a few seconds then got into the passenger seat as Simon settled into the driver's side.

"Don't fiddle with the seat adjustments, OK?" asked Yancey, "I may need to take over to do the fancy driving thing if something comes up."

Simon just grinned and said, "No prob. This is fine."

He glanced over and saw that his friend was asleep. Simon checked to make sure that Yancey had done up the five point seat belt properly before passing out, and then carefully pulled out and continued on.

It was getting dark when Simon pulled off into an unused picnic area to stop for supper, pulling off into some trees out of sight of the road. Yancey's eyes sprang open at the change in motion of the car, and he just managed to catch himself from attempting to spring forward. He turned to see Simon grinning broadly at him, "'Bout damn time you woke up, you lazy sod."

Yancey took a quick glance at the clock in the dashboard and frowned at his friend, "We were *supposed* to take turns driving. Where are we, exactly?"

Simon laughed and said, "Just west of Sleeping Giant Provincial Park. This seemed like a good spot to grab some food, stretch our legs, and decide what to do next."

Yancey had to admit the logic of that, so he unbuckled himself and got out of the car. Stomping around to loosen up, they surveyed the area.

Simon pointed, "The road's over there, and no-one's going to see us from it. Probably safe to have a light over at the picnic table over there. The fresh air feels good to me, if it's OK with you."

Once again, Yancey bowed to the wisdom of his friend. Together they rummaged in the back seat to emerge with a lantern, the food coolers and suitable cushions to sit on.

Setting up at the table, Simon observed that the previously hot foot was now barely warm. Yancey grinned and said, "Hey, you should have pulled over a couple of hours ago and put the stuff on top of the engine to heat it up."

Simon looked askance at his friend and could only say, "You've been watching 'Red Green' again, haven't you?"

The Christmas episode was a favorite of theirs.

Yancey had to laugh at the expression on his friend's face.

"No, no," he assured Simon, "It's a real thing! Been around for a long time. In fact, I added some hangers in the engine compartment for that very purpose. No, really! Here, grab the stuff in the foil containers and follow me. The engine's still hot, and a few minutes of heating will improve the food. Trust me."

Simon looked doubtful, but obeyed his friend's instructions. Popping up the hood of the Busted Flush, Yancey started arranging the covered containers at appropriate locations on the engine, then shut the hood.

"We'll give it about 10 or 15 minutes. It won't be really hot, but certainly warmer than it is now. Let's eat some of the salads and buns while we wait."

Returning to table, they dished themselves up some of the cold foods and started munching happily away. "Yum," enthused Simon, "I needed this. The only thing missing is coffee!"

Yancey offered to make some, but Simon demurred. "Water is fine, actually," he said, "We can make cocoa or something later, maybe."

They ate in silence for a few minutes.

"How's the gas holding out," asked Yancey.

"Pretty good," answered Simon, "But we'll need to get

some when we hit Thunder Bay."

A few more minutes passed as they finished their salads. Simon drummed his fingers on the table for a bit then said, "Let's see if the good stuff is hot enough to eat. I'm starved," and got up and headed for the car. Yancey followed him with a laugh.

Opening the hood, they retrieved the dishes from their resting places. They were actually too hot to hold comfortably, so they donned their gloves to carry the containers over to the table. Familiar odours greeted them when they opened up the containers. Not scalding hot, by any means, but certainly warm enough to be enjoyable. They quickly heaped their plates and dug in, happy to enjoy the good food and companionable silence.

Once the initial feeding frenzy had slowed down, Simon looked at Yancey as if he wanted to say something. He looked briefly down at his food, then looked back up.

"Yance, with all the stuff you've been telling me, I still get the impression that you're holding back something. You've left out the part about the Sword itself, so I'm thinking there's something about them that has you really worried."

Yancey looked at his friend and sighed, "Yeah, they scare me all right. I did some more reading and thinking about it while you were sleeping the other night. The attack the Sword made with the tank shows high grade training, outfitting, and intelligence. The planned attack on the Shattered Palace facility is even more aggressive and daring. Both are nation-state level stuff, not something a terrorist group is capable of doing. So I dug more into the material in Folder Four. I knew that something called 'Infinity Ascending' started being noticed around the 1900's. Think about that time. It was a time when the old established hierarchies and thought patterns were being challenged by new aggressive ones. Colonialism was at its peak, and strong men (always men, you'll notice) were carving out empires of their own. Empires of land as well as commerce. Socially, there was a head-on collision of beliefs - Darwinism, established religions, established aristocracies who felt themselves born to rule, and the new 'barons of commerce' who had elbowed their way into the halls of power. Add to this mix an unprecedented exponential increase in science and engineering, plus the demands of the 'lower orders' for a piece of the pie. The established elites saw their powers slipping away. The new elites wanted to hold on to what they'd acquired. Both of them wanted to continue or establish social controls that kept any competition in its place. This was the time when the secret societies of the elites were born, in Europe and North America - the Trilaterals, Bilderbergs, and others. Over time some merged, some changed their name, and some vanished. The 'Infinity Ascending' group was one of those that faded from view. They appear to have been a mixture of the commercial and social elites, with a strong religious component to bind them. They spoke of social controls, but via indirect rather than direct means. Then at some point they established something called the 'Sword of Infinity Ascending'. This apparently took a quasi-religious form, and was supposed to be the militant arm to do God's work along the path to ascension. Whatever that meant. After that group was formed, Infinity Ascending itself faded from sight. Even the Sword got rarely mentioned, but when it did it was for higher-end enforcement stuff, not the lower-end terrorist stuff. And it was always mentioned as being done for a path layed down by God. Very religious, very stern, very stark."

Yancey paused to peck at his food and drink some

water.

"Think about it, Simon. We've identified international cadres maneuvering to gain control of Canada on a political and economic level, but acting as influencers for the most part. We've got a group called the Sword of Infinity Ascending pulling off military attacks at the nation-state level of expertise and weaponry. You've identified the most aggressive of these maneuverings as coinciding with major historical economic and social conflicts."

Again Yancey paused.

Simon interjected, "Fine, but why hasn't anyone heard about these Sword bastards before now? Why now?"

Yancey looked at his friend, "That's what's got me scared. They've been around for a very long time, working behind the scenes, and obviously getting hooks into all sorts of places and at the highest levels, and now they're stepping out of the shadows. Politically, regressive forces are on the rise all over the world. Socially, there are enormous pressures to roll back individual rights in favour of enhanced corporate rights, and doing it quite successfully. The old 'know your place' mindset is coming back into vogue, along with unquestioning obedience to authority. Security and stability outweighing freedom. And now one of those groups wants weapons of mass destruction, and I think it's Infinity Ascending working through the Sword. It's like you said the other day, these groups are using Canada as a battleground. Well, now that battle has just gotten ramped up to the next level, and all of us are expendable. Less than expendable - we're not even worth noticing except as resources to be exploited. They're well-established with money, power, influence, agents in place, armies, weapons, everything."

Yancey was getting somewhat heated by the end of his

speech.

"So," said Simon, "Doesn't sound like a fair fight."

"Well, duh," answered Yancey, "They started it, so they'll just have to take their chances."

The two friends grinned at each other, then Simon raised his glass of water, "Illegitimi non carborundum."

Yancey raised his glass as well and repeated the toast with a matching lop-sided grin.

Both were silent for a handful of heartbeats, then Yancey spoke, "Well, that's settled. Now on to tactics. I'd kind of like to be further along than we are before we stop for the night. We could stop over in Thunder Bay, then get a fresh start in the morning, or we could carry on up to Highway 17 and hope to find something off the side of the road. The map doesn't show any rest areas along that stretch, so we'd probably have to pull over to the side of the road, or go up one of those minor roads and hope to find a place that we could pull over. That doesn't sound too appealing."

Simon stared at the map for a moment and pointed out that they could get WiFi access in Thunder Bay. Maybe check email.

Yancey stared off into the distance, thinking furiously, "No, I don't think that's wise."

He turned and looked at his friend, "The attack is imminent. Thunder Bay is the closest major centre, so it's bound to be covered by their agents. At the very least, they'll be monitoring all electronic communication very very closely. Too risky. Probably too risky to even rent a motel room there."

Simon raised an eyebrow at that.

"Think about it, Simon. Renting a room requires the use of a credit card, unless we get a really sleazy place, and those are going to be watched. Cash just raises too many questions these days, and gets noticed. We don't want to get noticed by anyone right now."

Yancey gnawed on a finger briefly, then sighed and said, "I think that right here is our best bet to spend the night. It's away from the road, we could even go a bit deeper into the trees if we wanted, and the bulk of the traveling from here is on highways, except for the final jog to the Shattered Palace. I think we should stay here for the night, spend some time going over our notes, and prepare our story and evidence to be presented to the military folks guarding the facility. If we leave just before dawn, that should get us to the facility before dark. Probably. With any luck."

He looked at Simon who simply shrugged and agreed.

"Do we make a proper fire for the night?" was Simon's only question.

Yancey looked around thoughtfully and responded sadly, "Nope. Its glow would be seen from the road. We don't have any proper sleeping bags, but I've got blankets and extra coats and some of those chemical hot pack things. We could even start up the Busted Flush every couple of hours to get some heat. Won't be overly cozy, but warm enough."

Simon agreed and they finished off their now-cool meal. Then they cleaned up and got the Busted Flush ready for the night.

They decided to take two hour shifts, starting up the car for ten minutes at every shift change, to add some heat and to charge up the electronics used by the one on guard. They spent some time discussing how to arrange their evidence, then began their wait for morning. Three shift changes passed, and then it was time to have breakfast and move on. They had a busy day ahead of them.

CHAPTER SIXTEEN
Into The Halls Of The Shattered Palace

Colonel Frederick Brown was unhappier than usual. It was the wee hours of the morning and he still had a couple more to go before the end of his watch. His second watch of the day, actually. Once again he cursed the absent Major Sam Ronsom, head of security, whose shift he was covering. And would continue to cover for the next week.

The Shattered Palace was normally blessed with a contingent of American special security forces to 'assist' the Canadians in guarding the weapons stored there. But somehow fortune had smiled on the Major and his forces, for they were off on a training seminar back in the United States. Col. Brown was glad that someone's career was still moving along enough that training seminars were granted. Although, come to think of it, it was only the American personnel who seemed to get the career-boosting training opportunities. Such opportunities were dispensed by the General, and it was simply not possible that such a high-ranking officer would play favorites. Or sabotage the careers of the soldiers of the host country. Unthinkable, especially for a senior officer of the General's level. Col. Brown snorted in disgust and cursed silently once more. It helped to pass the time.

What truly rankled was the way that the latest training issue had gone down. Two days ago he had been called into the General's office for a 'special briefing'. When he'd arrived, he found Maj. Ronsom standing there grinning like a cat who had just eaten a canary. The General was, as usual, sitting behind his regal-sized desk, sitting in his regal-sized specially-ordered chair, swiveling slowly back and forth. Col. Brown came to attention, snapped a sharp salute, and announced that he was present as per orders. The General glared balefully as he slowly swiveled back and forth. He believed it made him look dangerous and put the fear of God into anyone in his presence. The truth was it just made him look like a fool, and bored the hell out of all but the lowliest private. Brown waited patiently, for he'd played this game many times. Finally the General waved a vague salute, and Brown stood at parade ease. Not at real ease, for the General didn't like that, no not at all.

"Brown," said the General, for he rarely addressed the Major by his rank, "I have some good news for you and your men. A rare and great opportunity."

Brown's stomach sank. This was not going to be good.

The General continued, "Major Ronsom and the bulk of his team will be departing in a few hours to take part in an important training seminar. A well-deserved opportunity, I must say."

He nodded at Ronsom, whose chest puffed out even more.

"But sir," began Brown, "Protocol clearly states that the Major and his forces are to provide security for the nuclear weapons!"

The General waved away the remarks while continuing to swivel back and forth.

126

"Mere details, Brown, mere details. This is an important opportunity that cannot be missed for the Major and his team. It also affords the opportunity for you and your troops to step up to the plate and pull your weight, for a change. Demonstrate what you can do. You're always asking for more responsibility to be assigned to your troops, so here's your chance."

Major Ronsom spoke up, grinning, "Don't worry, Brown, I'll be leaving behind a corporal to hold your hands. Show your lot the ropes, as it were, and make sure that they don't do anything too stupid."

Col. Brown's eyes narrowed slightly at Ronsom's deliberate skipping of his rank.

"Quite so, Major, quite so," expounded the General, "Operationally, this means that you, as the Senior Canadian Officer, will be pulling the Major's shifts. On top of your regular duties, of course. Can't have you neglecting those."

Col. Brown said quietly and evenly, "Understood, sir. When are the Major and his men departing?"

"This evening," replied the General, "You and your second will be taking the Major's and his second's shift starting this evening."

Col. Brown stood there digesting this piece of wondrous news.

"Well don't just stand there, man, carry on, carry on. The Major can give you the keys and such before he leaves. He and I have important matters to discuss."

Col. Brown braced to attention, then turned and marched out of the room. Best to get out of there before he wrung both of their worthless necks, he thought.

As it was spoken, so it was done. He arranged with his second-in-command, Major Jean Frontenac, to cover the extra shifts in addition to their regular shifts. What should have been a simple, but useful, exercise in having everyone move up and take over the next rank's duties for a week had been turned into a farce. He and the Major decided to break up the extra shifts into three hour chunks, interspersing them throughout the day. That way one of them was always on call, but allowed for a bit of downtime for each. It was the best they could do.

Which explained why Col. Brown, on the last deployment of his long military career, was pulling a watch in the wee hours of the morning. The thought of that started him cursing again, but he stopped. Wouldn't do to be doing that so often that it lost its effectiveness, he thought. So he simply sighed and went back to reading the secret procedures manual that only the American security forces had access to. He had, of course, read and memorized it months before.

* * *

The last shift was Simon's, and at the end of it he woke up Yancey. "Time to get up, you lazy sod. It's the crack of dark and time to boogie."

Yancey woke up quickly, then got out of the car to do some quick stomping and stretching to get the kinks out. Simon had prepared a simple, cold breakfast which they both quickly consumed. After a brief break to pack up and answer the call of nature, they got into the car and were off with Yancey driving.

"We'll get some coffee when we stop for gas. Paying cash for that won't arouse any suspicions."

Both of them dearly missed their coffee.

"Get enough to fill a thermos or two," suggested Simon.

"Good idea," said Yancey yawning. "Shoulda thought of that. Hey, why don't you grab some sleep until we stop for gas?"

Simon allowed as that was a good idea and leaned back to doze. They arrived outside of Thunder Bay and stopped at a roadside gas bar. They gassed up the Flush, then stepped inside the coffee shop. There they ordered some breakfast food and coffee, to go. Then they decided to add some snack foods and pastries. The waitress behind the counter took their money, gave them their change, and got the order prepared. They took a few minutes to wolf down the breakfast food and gulp down some of the coffee, then they hit the road, eager to continue.

It wasn't too long before they arrived at the turnoff for Highway 17. Yancey was still driving while Simon was looking at maps again. He had a couple of paper maps out, plus a map program running on his laptop. None of them agreed with each other, of course, but that was normal enough. "OK" said Simon finally, "Keep going for, uhm, fifty kilometers or so. There's a not-too-small road marked on two of the three maps that heads north and continues pretty far along."

Several hours, and many kilometers of bumpy back roads later, they were forced to come to a halt. The road they were on ended as it intersected a road running east and west, but not north. The silence in the car was somewhat strained. They were some distance away from where they needed to be, with no obvious route available to get there.

"So where to now, oh great navigator," inquired Yancey with strained politeness.

Simon looked up from his maps with a frazzled look on his face. "AAAAAAAH," he screamed in reply.

Yancey waited for the echos of the scream to die out in the close confines of the car. In truth he didn't blame his friend. It was a secret facility, after all, and had remained so for decades. So where was it? He put the car in park, and got out to look around. There was very little variety in the landscape, just the usual northern Ontario gently rolling hills of stone with scraps of vegetation clinging to it here and there. Interspersed was the occasional outcropping of forest. Ahead of them was one of billions of low rocky hills. Stretching east and west was another minor road. He could see for kilometers down the road, and there was no sign of any turnoff anywhere.

Suddenly he heard a soft mechanical buzzing sound, getting closer fairly rapidly. He got back in the car. "Buckle up tight," he told Simon, "Someone's coming."

They both quickly cinched up their restraints. Yancey put the car into gear and slowly headed west, just for the sake of appearing to be moving. He looked in his rear view mirror and saw two three-wheeled forest bikes roaring up at high speed. "Bogies incoming at six o'clock. Get ready to wave and look friendly."

The two motor bikes were strangely quiet as they rushed towards them, and slowing down only slightly the black-clad rider on each pointed their hands at the Busted Flush and suddenly flames spat out of their hands, followed by a loud boom.

"Guns! They're firing guns at us," yelled Simon.

Yancey didn't answer, but spun the steering wheel around and aimed the car in the opposite direction while stepping on the accelerator. The two motor bikes slowed, then quickly followed. Yancey's speed was limited because of the coating of snow on top of the poor quality of the dirt road, but that didn't seem to bother the bikes. They quickly gained on the car, and then started firing their pistols again. The Busted Flush didn't waver as the slugs thudded into its body. The bikes began roaring up, one to either side, and the pistols were aimed again. This time at the windows. The guns spat flame just as Yancey flung the Busted Flush around in a tight skidding turn, foot still on the accelerator to maintain speed. The tires lost traction on the dirt road, and the car spun a couple of complete revolutions before skidding off the road and onto one of the rocky hills, moving upwards. But not before slamming against each of the attackers. The weight of the car, and its momentum, flung both of the attackers against the rocks on either side. They hit hard and dropped, not to rise again. The Busted Flush, meanwhile, continued nearly to the top before finally skidding to a halt.

"Why aren't we dead" muttered Simon. Then much more loudly and rapidly, "YANCEY WHY AREN'T WE DEAD THEY WERE SHOOTING AT US WHY AREN'T WE DEAD?"

Yancey sat there with his hand firmly gripping the steering wheel for several heartbeats before answering, "The Flush used to be a police car, remember?"

Then he barked out a laugh, "The Kevlar lining is still there. And I beefed up the windows a few years back."

He looked around at a couple of spiderwebs of cracks on the windows. He fumbled at the restraints, then hopped out of the car. Simon quickly followed. Both were still panting from the excitement.

They looked down onto the road and saw the twisted bodies of their attackers. Then they looked at the Busted Flush, and saw the carefully placed bullet holes in the sides. Simon spoke first, carefully and quietly, "Defenders or Sword?"

Yancey looked down carefully, standing perfectly still lest he slip on the snow-covered rock. He could see the tire tracks of the Flush as it had churned around the road and up the low slope. "Look at the suits they're wearing. That's not standard issue for any military I've ever heard about. Still, could be special forces of some sort I suppose."

He turned carefully and went back to the driver's side door, and extracted a short tube. Extending it he held it up to his eye and twisted it into focus. He gazed thoughtfully for a few seconds then passed it to Simon. "Look at the shoulder patch," was all he said.

Simon looked where he was instructed and saw dark gray symbol that looked like a somewhat-distorted number eight. "Oh shit," breathed Simon.

Yancey had gotten his breathing under control, and his voice was measured and controlled once again. "Probably a scouting party or perimeter patrol of some sort. We're close to the facility, within about ten kilometers, I think. If that's a Sword patrol, then the attack is either taking place or imminent."

He turned carefully once again and walked upwards past the car and to the top of the ridge. "We're a bit higher here, so may as well take a look around."

He trudged up to the top of the hill and stopped. Then he laughed and pointed just ahead, "There's the secret road that we were looking for!"

Simon scrambled up carefully and looked. There was stretch of good road, sweeping northwards, towards their destination. He looked around and added a laugh of his own "Hey, look, if we just keep going over the top and down, we should be able to get to the road! It'll be bumpy going down, and slippery. Can the Flush handle that?"

"Watch and learn, little buddy, watch and learn," was the reply.

With that, they re-entered the car and buckled up. "Wait a minute," said Simon, "Should we go and get their guns and stuff?"

"No," replied Yancey, "If that's Future Soldier type

equipment then it'll all be keyed to authorized soldiers to prevent hostiles (that's us, by the way) from using it. No, we need to get going as quickly as possible to the facility."

And with that he started the car, put it into its lowest gear and carefully completed the climb to the top of the rocky hill, and then just as carefully down. When they reached the road he stepped on the throttle until they were roaring ahead as quickly as they could on the snowy highway. They knew that time was short.

* * *

Major Frontenac was trying very hard to control his temper, and barely succeeding. He and his troops were manning the security stations around the facility because all the American security 'experts' had decide to go off for a bit of fun. All but one of them, anyways, and that corporal was the cause of his anger.

"Corporal Jamison," Frontenac said clearly and softly, "Our perimeter sensors have picked up several gunshots. Would it be too much to ask for you to assist us to triangulate the source? And quickly."

"Why shore, Chief. No need to get yer undies in a knot," Jamison said with a broad Texas drawl,"Prob'ly jest hunters out fer some sport. Same as always."

Major Frontenac speared Jamison with a steely glare, "The rank is Major," he said softly, with the hint of emphasis on the rank. He'd been putting up with this sort of disrespect for a very long time, and this was not the time or place to be testing his patience.

"Shore thing, Chief," Jamison said with a grin that bordered on a sneer, "All ya'll gotta do is switch in the differentiators and auto-DSP analyzers. Don't rightly know why you insist on doin' everything in manual mode anyways."

Major Frontenac walked slowly towards the corporal, being careful not to touch him. That would be against regulations. But the rage was evident in his eyes, and Jamison instinctively backed up until he was against a wall. Frontenac moved his face to within a centimeter of the other's and said softly but intently, "The RANK is MAJOR. You will remember that. You will use that when addressing me. If not, there will be consequences. Do. You. Understand. Me."

The tone of the Major's voice clearly indicated that it was not a question.

Jamison knew that he had pretty much pushed his luck as far as he could with the powerfully built officer. "Yessir, Major, sir."

This exchange was interrupted by one of the Canadian soldiers monitoring the systems. "Sir! Another contact! One vehicle inbound along the main road. Traveling at sixty klicks per hour."

Frontenac dashed to the security station to look at the displays. Jamison quietly let out the breath that he'd been holding.

"Details," barked Frontenac.

"System says that the engine sounds like a civilian V8. Visual and IR make it out as a large sedan. Should be here in a couple of minutes," the soldier replied.

Frontenac grabbed a phone and dialed a number to alert the guard posts. Then he dialed up Colonel Brown's number. He didn't want to interrupt the Colonel's much-needed rest but this was something he'd want to see himself.

* * *

The Busted Flush traveled up the roadway as quickly as Yancey dared. The attack by the Sword patrol probably meant that the attack was imminent.

"Yance, over there," Simon said excitedly pointing ahead and to the left, "Where the road swings behind that line of trees. Looks like a dead end or parking zone or something. One of the secondary entrance portals was supposed to be nearby, I think."

Yancey began slowing the car down a bit. The road was too slippery for sudden maneuvers. They quickly reached the bend in the road and coasted to a stop. The road seemed to end here, in a small cleared area surrounded by trees. They looked at each other, then back outside. "I guess we get out here and look around," suggested Simon.

"I guess," responded Yancey. "OK, let's hook up and bail out. Oh, grab those packs with the evidence in them, will you?"

Simon turned around and grabbed two small backpacks. He tossed one to Yancey and kept the other. They unbuckled their safety harnesses and climbed out. Their breath streamed around them in the chilly air. Yancey pointed. "Over there, I think."

And off they trudged.

Within a minute they'd found a small structure with a door. They'd almost missed it at first, it being only a couple meters high and blending in perfectly with the surroundings, especially with the snow on top of everything. It was a very sturdy looking door, with no obvious knobs or controls in sight.

They looked at the door, then each other, then back at the door.

"Now what?" asked Simon. "Seems just a tad anti-climatic, doesn't it?"

"That it does. Well, we've got to assume that we're being watched. So let's be polite and knock."

With that Yancey stepped forward and carefully rapped the door with his knuckles as if this was a regular house. After a few seconds he said, "No-one seems to be at home. Or maybe they're not answering the door today."

Yancey stepped back a couple of paces and stood facing the door. "Hello," he began, "My name is Yancey Franklin, and this is my friend Simon Thane."

Simon raised his arm and gave a little wave as Yancey continued, "We've come a long way to warn you about an impending attack on your facility. We ran into a couple of the Bad Guys at the other end of your road there, just over the hill at the end of it, and I strongly suspect that their associates are on their way here."

The lack of any response was making Yancey feel more than a little foolish. They looked at each other and Simon shrugged. He opened his mouth to speak just as a sound could be heard coming from behind the door. Both of them jumped back a pace in surprise, unwilling to say anything.

The unidentifiable sound became more distinct, like a large pipe valve being turned with the addition of random thumps.

"You will both stand very still," a strong and distinct voice declared from somewhere behind them, "We are authorized to use deadly force. Place your hands on top of your heads and interlock your fingers."

Yancey and Simon obeyed quickly.

"Now get on your knees and keep your hands on your heads."

Once again they obeyed. As soon as they had complied with the order, they were seized by strong hands and rendered immobile.

"Area secure," the voice declared again.

This time the door opened quickly and silently to show

three armed soldiers. Their rifles were at the ready, but not aimed at the prisoners. Once opened, the ordinary-looking door looked almost as thick as the door on a small bank vault.

The hands holding them immobile stripped their backpacks off, then raised the two friends to their feet. Their coats were quickly removed, and their belts, with the attached pouches, cut off. After a brief but thorough pat down, their hands were handcuffed behind their backs and they were turned around to face their captors.

They saw four soldiers in camouflaged uniforms, all but one holding a rifle at the ready. The other soldier was holding a pistol, also at the ready. The faces of all were alert, wary, but professional.

The soldier with the pistol said to the others, "We'll go through the main portal. The Colonel will want to interrogate them as quickly as possible."

With that he turned around, holstered his sidearm, and strode quickly away. The other soldiers followed at the same pace, firmly pulling Yancey and Simon forward with them.

They walked through another group of trees and then saw a structure similar to the one they'd just seen, but larger and sturdier. The door was open, and this one looked like the door of a large bank vault. They walked in without pause and as they entered, the door closed behind them. Silently, quickly, and with the smallest of thumps as it was sealed.

They marched a few dozen meters down a corridor and then into a small empty room. Firm hands held them in the centre, and then someone brought in a couple of plain, wooden chairs. They were forced down onto the chairs, and their captors left without saying a word.

"Well," said Yancey brightly, "We've made contact.

D'you think we should ask to be taken to their leader?"

"All in all," sighed Simon, "I don't think they've got much of a sense of humour."

Time passed without any more idle banter. Finally Simon inquired, "How long has it been? They've had enough time to examine our belongings and take a quick look at the evidence we brought, or at least the printouts. Time's short, Yancey."

"Yeah," Yancey replied quietly, "It's been, oh, twenty or thirty minutes anyways. We might want to think about making a fuss pretty soon. Like you say, time's getting short. But I don't want to piss them off. That'll just delay things, and time is something we just don't have. Let's give it a few more minutes, but no more."

Within a few seconds the door opened. A pair of soldiers came inside the room while two more waited outside. Without a word Yancey and Simon were raised to their feet and into the corridor. They were marched along a few dozen meters, then steered into another short corridor and into another room. This room was somewhat larger, and reasonably well lit, with a table and several chairs. The two chairs behind the table were occupied by two hard-looking soldiers. Officers, by the look of them, Yancey thought. On the table was their backpacks, pouches, and remains of their belts. There were two empty chairs in front of the table. Their guards marched them to those chairs and forced them to sit, then stood behind them. Very intimidating, very professional thought Yancey. Simon's thoughts were less sanguine. Both tried very hard to project calmness, and for the most part succeeded.

One of the soldiers behind the desk, the older of the two, looked at Yancey and said, "You are Yancey Franklin."

He turned to Simon and said, "You are Simon Thane."

It was a statement, not a question. Both nodded.

The older officer continued, "Each of you was carrying two pouches and a knife. A rather well-designed small combat knife, not the usual department store kind."

He paused briefly to indicate the items in question. "Each of you had one pouch with a nice little survival kit, and one pouch with a pair of data sticks. Your backpacks had similar, but not identical contents. One had several inches worth of printouts and several CD's, and the other held a laptop computer along with several CD's and data sticks."

As before, he was making statements, not asking questions.

"You arrived and stated that you had been attacked, and that some force was about to stage an attack on this facility."

Again, a statement.

Then the first question, "Describe the attackers and their weapons." It was delivered in a mild, but thoroughly professional tone that assumed obedience.

Yancey licked his lips and described where the attack took place, the two Sword soldiers who had attacked them, and the pistols they used.

"The only reason that you are here and not in a holding cell is that our security system did detect pistol shots originating in that area. But yours was the only vehicle. Why?"

Yancey explained about the silenced trail bikes. "Possibly electric, but I don't know for certain. We didn't examine the vehicles or the soldiers after the fight."

The older officer raised one eyebrow and tilted his head slightly, inviting Yancey to continue.

Yancey took a deep breath. The real conversation was about to begin.

"Because according to the documentation we had obtained, the enemy forces have advanced body armour and weaponry that would undoubtedly be locked against misuse. Also, we knew that some sort of attack was being planned against this facility and very soon. The presence of those troops guarding the perimeter indicated that the attack was imminent. We decided that time was of the essence, and that warning you was our first priority."

The face examining Yancey grew colder and harder, as did his tone, "And why did you assume that those were 'enemy' soldiers, and not ours? We have patrols out. With silenced vehicles."

Yancey did not whither under that stare, "Because, sir, they wore the uniforms of the Sword of Infinity Ascending. If they were using your vehicles then I'm afraid they took them from your patrol."

The two officers sat upright as if struck. The younger one almost leapt to his feet, but was restrained with a glance by his elder.

"Explain," said the older officer in a voice of ice and steel.

"Sir," began Yancey, "I'm sure you've at least glanced at the printed material we brought?"

He was rewarded with a terse nod.

"You've seen the intelligence file about this facility? It was on the top."

Again a terse nod.

Yancey licked his lips and took a deep breath, "Someone with very very good connections has compiled a detailed description of this facility, its security systems, and personnel. The purpose, as outlined in those captured documents, is to steal the nuclear and biological weapons that are stored here, then cover up the crime by blowing up the chemical weapons and contaminating the entire area."

Yancey paused for breath and continued in a rush, "Everything we've uncovered indicates that the attack is being carried out by the Sword of Infinity Ascending, the same group that attacked Toronto. And that attack is to take place during a very specific five day window, starting from yesterday. I don't know why that time window is important, but the documents are very specific."

Colonel Brown and Major Frontenac looked at each other. They could take a very good guess as to the reason for that window.

They were interrupted by a knock on the door, and a soldier came in, saluted and passed a folder to the officers, then left.

Col. Brown examined the contents of the folder for a couple of minutes then looked up, "Mr. Franklin, it says here that you are a private detective. Not a terribly successful one, at least financially, but with some surprising successes in some rather offbeat cases. And you, Mr. Thane, were until recently employed as a data analyst specializing in what could be called 'business intelligence'."

He paused for a moment and passed the file to his subordinate who examined it carefully. After a moment looking at the two young men, he motioned to their guards and said, "Uncuff them."

Frontenac looked up sharply at that order but Brown just nodded briefly to him.

"My name is Colonel Brown, and this is Major Frontenac," he said quietly, "Thank you for your warning."

Yancey grinned and said, "Ah yes, the Senior Canadian Officer, and your second-in-command."

Brown grunted. "You do your homework, young man."

Then he turned to the Major and said, "The guards are already on alert. But let's bring them up to Full Alert status, and put extra troops at the portals. We can call it a drill if the General asks. Speaking of whom, I'd better let him know what's going on."

Major Frontenac grinned and saluted, then turned to leave to carry out his orders.

* * *

General Thomas Thansworth the Third was sitting quietly in his chair, his breathing slow and controlled. This had been part of his daily routine for many years, but these days he was having to do it several times a day. Maybe it was the depressingly drab paint scheme used throughout the facility. Maybe it was small rooms. Maybe it was the ceilings that always seemed too low. This damned facility just seemed so damn *small*, and the thought of the weight of all that soil above his head always made his skin crawl.

If only he could take his medicine, then it would all seem alright, at least for a while. But he had no medicine any more. Not since before he was sent here. Back in the Good Times, when his rank and family name were enough to garner him the respect he craved, expected, and demanded. Just one little incident, he thought savagely, it was just the one time that he got caught. And it was so soon after the warning, too. That was the problem. No-one had gotten hurt. No-one that mattered, anyway. But that was not how the Board saw it. It was only because of his family's connections that he was spared a full inquiry, and he knew that would be the end of his cherished military career.

It had come out of the blue, the offer to command a special secret base, and a great surprise to him. A small base, to be sure, but the allure of secrecy made it all the more appealing. And the name 'Shattered Palace' hinted at wonders and secrets that could mean the resurrection of his career. Ignoring the multi-year enforced length of the posting, he had accepted the offer. It did not take so very long after arriving that he renamed the facility 'Poisoned Chalice."

Not that he ever said that out loud. Oh, no. Ears would hear, and tongues would wag, and the bastards who had set him up would learn of it. No, better to never speak of it, and never give them the satisfaction of seeing his pain or knowledge of his suffering.

The worst of it was being reduced to commanding a force of foreigners. Worse, foreigners who refused to acknowledge his rightful leadership. Oh they obeyed the forms correctly enough, but their eyes showed their true feelings. Oh yes. And he hated them for it. For being part of his undeserved punishment.

His breathing was faster now as he lost the mantra of calmness, and the memories of pain and shame flooded in once again. And the walls, those damnable walls felt like they were closing in again.

His reverie was interrupted by the buzzing of his telephone. Thansworth jerked upright, prepared to unleash his wrath on the fool who had interrupted him. He picked up the phone and snarled a demand for identification. The voice on the other end spoke with a Texas drawl, but the words came out quickly. Thansworth grew rigid with fury. "You did well to inform me of this. Thank you, Corporal," he said when the voice grew silent.

He replaced the phone carefully, then stood up. Some outsiders had been captured outside of his facility and those bloody foreign *fools* … he wouldn't honour them with the term 'soldiers' … hadn't thought to inform him.

He was going to have to set them straight. Again. Bloody incompetents.

* * *

Major Frontenac had just reached the door when it was flung open and General Thansworth burst into the room.

"What the *hell* is going on here?" he barked out loudly, "Why was I not informed immediately?"

Brown and Frontenac had both come to attention and saluted. Simon and Yancey just stood there. Simon looked started. Yancey looked faintly amused - he'd read the background information on the General.

"Sir!" replied Col. Brown, "I was just about to call you. These gentlemen here arrived with some important information that I was looking into before calling you. A hostile force is ..."

"I don't give a damn what you think you know, Brown," yelled Thansworth, "I will not tolerate your disrespect and attempts to undermine my authority!"

With that he turned to the two guards standing next to Simon and Yancey and commanded, "Take these prisoners to a holding cell immediately."

"Sir, if I may ... " began Colonel Brown.

He was overridden by Thansworth almost immediately, "Be silent!"

Thansworth was almost quivering with anger, his face flushed and sweating. He then turned to the confused guards, "You have your orders! I said IMMEDIATELY!"

The guards saluted, their faces a study in stone. "Sir!" was all they said before they took the arms of the prisoners and marched them out the door.

Turning back to the Colonel, the General continued, "As for you, Brown, my patience with your insubordination is at an end. I will, by God, have you broken for this!"

The General's voice became louder and more shrill as he continued. The Colonel had seen him go off on rants before, but never this bad. The only thing to do, he had learned, was to stand quietly until the General wound down and dismissed him. By tomorrow it would be forgotten. It always was.

The General's diatribe was interrupted by a shrill alarm, followed by the public address system blaring "Colonel Brown to Security. Colonel Brown to Security. Hostile forces detected and incoming."

All three officers looked at each other then turned to the door. The General shoved the other two aside to ensure that he was first through the door. The other two officers just looked at each other and shook their heads. The situation looked too serious to worry about the General's tantrums.

* * *

The soldiers guarding them led Simon and Yancey deeper into the facility. As they turned a corner of the winding corridor, they encountered two more soldiers. A man and a woman. They stopped to give the larger party room to pass, and stared intently.

Just then the alarm shrieked, and the intercom paged Colonel Brown to Security. The two soldiers holding the prisoners stopped and looked at each other with indecision. They knew full well how understaffed they were at the moment, and that their commanding officer - their *real* commanding officer - did not see these prisoners as a threat. Still, orders were orders. Then one of the soldiers, the senior of the two, turned to the new soldiers and said, "We need to get to our duty stations! The General ordered these two to be locked up in the holding cell, but the Colonel was thanking them for warning us about an impending attack. Looks like it's started! Can you take care of these two for us?"

With that the two guards released Yancey and Simon, and ran back down the hallway.

Yancey and Simon looked at the two new soldiers, who were looking back at them. "Uhm," said the man, "I'm Corporal Fleming, and this is Private Landry. What's this about an attack?"

Yancey looked at the arms of the soldiers and saw that Fleming's rank-badge had a shiny spot where a third stripe once was. Similarly, Landry's rank-badge showed a spot where two other stripes had once been. Both had a large number of specialist badges. Not ordinary low-rankers, then, Yancey thought.

"We think it's the Sword of Infinity Ascending," Yancey said simply. Simon looked sharply at him, but Yancey just shrugged in reply.

Both of the soldiers jerked as if hit. They knew that name, and what it could mean.

Before they could say anything more, there was the sound of explosions from the direction of the portals, and then the alarms began shrieking.

The four of them looked around, then at each other. Landry opened his mouth to speak, and then the sound of the automatic doors closing began to reach them.

* * *

The Security Control Room was crowded. Never a large room, it now had all three of the senior officers in it. The General seemed to take up enough space for any three men.

"What's the situation?" the General barked.

"Sir, we've got hostiles ..." began a Canadian soldier at the central station.

"Not you, you idiot," barked the General, "You," pointing at Corporal Jamison.

Jamison was somewhat wild-eyed, but with excitement or fear no-one could tell.

"Sir! Hostile troops have captured Aux Portal One! Mebbe a hunert of 'em, can't rightly tell. Another large force is a-headin' fer the Main Portal. Aux Portal Two is clear of the buggers. They don't seem to know about it. But they've taken out the outside cameras so we can't rightly tell what those devils are up to!"

Jamison was panting by the end of his report.

"Sir, we need to assemble our forces to defend the facility," Colonel Brown began.

"Oh, shut up Brown," sneered the General, "This is no time for amateurs. Leave this to the professionals."

With that he turned to Jamison, "Son, what's our defensive situation?"

"Sir! Aux Portal One has been opened from the outside!" stated the Canadian soldier at the central station.

Suddenly there was an explosion, closely followed by several more.

The General did not bother to berate him. He was too busy breathing heavily, almost panting. The room was so small. So dreadfully small.

"Main Portal has been opened from the outside!"

Suddenly more alarms began shrieking. The General was tempted to shriek along with them, but managed to control himself and yell, "What is happening?"

Jamison yelled, "Fire! Those bastards must have started fires when they breached the portals! We're trapped in here! Trapped!"

He was almost shrieking by the end of his report.

The display board lit up with flashing lights, that seemed to travel in a wave through the facility.

"What's that?" the General yelled, his voice rising.

"Internal security doors are closin'!" Jamison was shrieking now, "They're trappin' us in here! We's gonna burn! We's gonna burn!"

The General's eyes took on the panicked look of a trapped animal. "NO!" he yelled, "LOOK!" and he pointed at the display, "The corridor to Aux Portal Two is clear! We can evacuate through there!"

His eyes were bright with triumph. He was saved!

"SIR!" yelled Colonel Brown, "NO! We cannot abandon the facility! We must defend it!"

The General grabbed Brown's uniform by the front and shook him, then roared, "I HAVE GIVEN THE ORDER TO EVACUATE AND IT WILL BE OBEYED!"

He tossed Brown backwards, then shook himself. "We will evacuate in good order and call the base in North Bay for reinforcements. That is protocol, *Colonel*. That is the plan as prepared by professionals, *Colonel*. Those are my orders, and you will see to it that they are obeyed."

He then turned to Jamison and said "Order all personnel to evacuate through Aux Portal Two immediately. Immediately!"

Jamison turned to his station and gleefully began broadcasting the command to evacuate.

Colonel Brown was too stunned to respond to this foolishness that bordered on insanity. How could the General abandon the facility in the face of a hostile force of unknown strength? Without even an attempt at defending it? Protocol called for a strong defense before calling in the forces stationed at North Bay.

"Sir! All outside communication lines are down!" yelled one of the soldiers from his console.

The Colonel turned to face the General, "Sir! We must stay to defend the facility. We cannot raise North Bay!"

The General was having none of it it. He pushed Brown away with a snarl and grabbed a microphone. Signaling to Jamison, he broadcast to the entire facility, "This is General Thansworth. I have given the order to evacuate the facility via Aux Portal Two. This is not a drill. You have your orders."

He tossed aside the microphone, not caring where it landed. That had been his first command given in a real battle. It felt good, but not good enough to drown out the need to get out of the small rooms that were pressing in on him more and more. He turned and fled the room, followed by all the other soldiers.

"Sir!" yelled Major Frontenac over the din of the alarms, "We still have people trapped behind some of those doors!"

"I know!" replied Brown, "But we have to control the evacuation or else it will become a panic! Make sure that our troops grab weapons on their way out! And a radio so that we can call for reinforcements! Go! I'll do a quick sweep for stragglers!"

He gave the Major a light shove to get him moving and looked quickly around the room. He looked at the monitors showing the destruction of his command and snarled briefly. He hurriedly gathered up a few items, then ran out of the room.

The General had always been a firm believer in leading from the front. And so it was that he was the first person to exit the Shattered Palace. But he was quickly followed by a trickle, and then a stream of soldiers running behind him as he led them directly away from the Palace.

Plumes of smoke rose into the air, as if to signal the death of sleeping dreams.

CHAPTER SEVENTEEN
Go Tell The Spartans

Master Corporal Jaques DuBois carefully surveyed the handful of soldiers before him. Until last week he'd been a Sergeant, but his stripe had been pulled (again) for insubordination. But the troops still thought of him as a sergeant, and he was the senior rank right now anyways.

"What sorts of weapons do we have?" he asked quietly.

It turned out that it wasn't as bad as it could have been, but most certainly not enough to effectively defend the site. Every one of the eight troopers had at least one pistol, several had two, and at least 8 full reloads for each pistol. In addition, there were 4 grenades and a few flash-bangs. And the usual assortment of knives, garrotes, and hatchets.

"Sergeant, I mean, Master Corporal, do you know what we're facing?" said one of the troopers.

"It's not good," began DuBois, "The installation has been infiltrated by at least a dozen hostiles. They control access to Aux Portal One and the main portal. Each is wearing a high-tech armour system and carrying heavy weapons. They seem to have pass cards and passwords to pretty much every sector, and their weapons can open up anything the pass cards can't. The good news is that they seem to be traveling as a group, and are either unaware of the security cameras or simply don't care. Given that most of the staff including the security combat teams have evacuated the installation, the latter is probably the case."

"Sir, why did the General order a complete evacuation? He knows what's stored here! Is he planning to re-group and attack?" queried one of the troopers.

"I dunno the answer to that one," DuBois quietly said, "All I know is that he ordered a complete bug out of personnel, administrative and security. As far as I can determine only small-arms were taken with them, nothing heavier than a standard battle rifle. There's no way he can mount an effective counter-attack with that. So my guess is that the Yanks ran out and plan to keep running. Us even talking about staying could be considered disobeying a direct order. But someone *has* to defend this place! The only reason for the hostiles to be here is to take the nukes and germs, and I cannot allow that to happen. The fucking Yanks may have dumped that shit here, but now we're stuck with making sure that it stays secure. No matter what. Maybe the General is planning a counter-attack. Maybe more troops are on the way. I hope to God that's the case. But someone has to contain and hold the hostiles before they reach the Treasure Vault. And that's us, lads and lassies."

MCpl. DuBois looked carefully at each of the eight soldiers in his squad. An odd mixture, but par for the Palace he thought to himself. Each one of us labeled as malcontents and sent here to end out our careers in the dead-end black hole that was the Shattered Palace.

"Anyone who cares to obey the direct order of the General to evacuate is free to do so," DuBois stated.

No-one moved. All of them sneered at the mention of the General and his orders. A few spat.

"OK," said DuBois, "Let's get this reception committee organized. I've got a remote display from the Security Office, so we can track the hostiles. Their path has to come straight down corridor Charlie-56, and that's got no exits until they hit the intersection with corridor Foxtrot-3. That's where we'll set up our defensive line. Charlie-56 curves here, so they'll have a bit of cover. Here's what we need to grab from this location before we head out to the intersection. With any luck we can hold them for a good long time."

* * *

The computer room was cool and quiet, with only the hum of the air conditioners to break the silence. The only inhabitants were two privates whose assignment was to tend to the obsolete mainframes like acolytes serving forgotten gods in a forgotten temple. The tedium of their devotions broken only by D&D games, since non-official electronic devices were forbidden within the Palace.

"Jeezus, Goldie, how are we going to get out of here? The hostiles are between us and the exits!" moaned Pte. Jason Philips.

"Well, how the fuck should I know?" spat his friend, Pte. Samuel Goldstein, "Maybe they'll ignore us. They gotta be terrorists or something. Who knows what they want? How the hell did they even know about the Palace?"

Both were silent for a moment.

"Jase, you know its gotta be the Treasure Vault they're after," Pte. Goldstein quietly opined, "I mean, if they're terrorists, those old nuclear warheads and bioweapons have got to be a pretty tempting target. That's all we've got here! I mean, these computers hold data that's older than us! Nothing secret. Nothing worth launching an armed assault for!"

Pte. Philips was thinking furiously. "Actually, it's worse than that," he said, "Look at the security feeds. They're wearing some sort of high-tech armour system, like what the American army has been experimenting with for years. And those rifles of theirs! They shoot bullets but also what looks like grenades of some sort. Nasty shit. And no sounds from the soldiers! No hand signals or orders being spoken, so they've got to have some sort of squad-level radio communications built into those helmets. The teargas and smoke bombs didn't even slow them down, so their helmets are sealed and have IR vision or something built in. Very sophisticated. Very dangerous."

Pte. Goldstein was typing furiously at his keyboard. "Looks like everyone but us has managed to bug out after the General issued the evac order. Oh, wait! There's a few holdouts. Hmm, looks like some of ours are heading to intercept the hostiles at the first intersection. Holy fuck, what are they going to be able to do against that sort of firepower? Thanks to that fucktard General, we've got nothing but small arms and not much of that! Everything good is locked up and out of reach!"

Pte. Philips was also typing furiously. "Looks like some of ours are in the Treasure Vault. Maybe they can lock it down. It's built like a bank vault, only better!"

"Don't be too sure about that, Jase," said his friend, "The hostiles got through the outer doors without a problem, which means they've got access to some if not all the passkeys and pass codes. And the doors they didn't have keys for they just blew open with no problem. That means some seriously modern boom-tech. I wouldn't count on the vault doors holding them for very long."

"Which brings me to my original questions, Goldie -

what are we going to do?"

Pte. Philips had gotten a grip on his initial fear, but couldn't keep a quaver out of his voice, "We're just computer nerds! We failed Basic Training, but got sent here anyways after we posted those pictures of the Commandant after the Christmas party. Shit on a stick, Sam, neither of us have ever managed to fire a rifle without hurting ourselves, much less hit a target!"

"Wrong," whispered his friend, "We're soldiers. Canadian soldiers. It doesn't matter why we're here. It doesn't matter what our assignment here is. We're soldiers. Our duty station is being invaded by hostiles whose obvious intent is to take some of the most horrible weapons ever developed and turn them against people ... civilians ... *our* civilians. We can't just sit here and do nothing."

"Maybe the force at the intersection will stop them," Pte. Philips said hopefully.

"Not going to happen," said Pte. Goldstein sadly, "Our guys will slow them down, sure, and maybe take some of them out. Hell, if Frenchy DuBois is there then it's goddamn sure that some of the hostiles will be taken out. But the hostiles have superior numbers and weapons. At some point they'll eliminate the force at the intersection and head for the Treasure Vault. And to get there they'll be coming right by us. But I'll be damned if I can think of a way to do anything to slow them down, much less stop them. Somehow I don't think they'll be too impressed with our hacker skills and level 60 D&D characters."

"OK, so we're soldiers," said Pte. Philips tonelessly, "But we better think of something really brilliant really fast. The hostiles are approaching the intersection."

* * *

Yancey and Simon looked around in amazement. Their two guides are dragged them along with them in the hurried flight after the announcement of the attack and subsequent order to evacuate.

"Geez, Yance, this all looks like something out of that movie 'Dr. Strangelove'," exclaimed Simon.

"Not too surprising," said Cpl. Fleming with a slight smile, "It was designed and built about that time."

"This is all very fascinating," said Yancey carefully, "But shouldn't we be evacuating along with everyone else?"

"Well, first of all there are only two exits out of the Palace available from here," explained Pte. Landry, "One was disabled during the initial assault, and the other seems to be the route the hostiles are taking. There's one more that was used for the evacuation but we can't get to it."

"Secondly," continued Cpl. Fleming, "The hostiles will be heading here. In case you haven't noticed, this is what we called the Treasure Vault. Remember that? This is where all that delightfully obscene nuclear and biowar hardware is stored. This has got to be what the hostiles want, and we can't allow that. We may not agree with why this facility exists, or what it is being used to store, but our duty is crystal clear — we must prevent the hostiles from getting their hands on this. At all costs."

"But what, exactly, can we do," asked Yancey. "The only weapons that I can see are the pistols you two are carrying. Simon and I will do what we can, but we're not soldiers. I've got a bit of training with pistols, but Simon's never fired a gun in his life. Those doors we passed through are thicker than any bank vault I've ever heard of, so won't those be enough to stop the intruders?"

Pte. Landry shook her head, "The hostiles seem to have gotten through all of our defenses, both physical and electronic with ease. That means they know how to neutralize them or have all the necessary access codes and keys. I doubt they've come all this way to be stopped by the vault doors, I really don't."

"Molly, can I get your help to check the stock?" requested Cpl. Fleming, "The quick-look check says that everything is in place, but we need to activate the full check procedure before we can start thinking about any sort of lockdown."

"Sure," said Pte. Landry, "I'll start up the check-weigh system."

Suddenly, the distant thud of explosions were faintly heard.

* * *

"CONTACT!" yelled Pte. Bolten as he fired a round at a fast-moving figure from behind a hastily-constructed barricade.

"OK, lads and lassies, look alive," declared MCpl. DuBois, "We've not got ammunition to waste, so make every shot hit a hostile. They're well armoured so if you can, hit the helmet or the legs. Just make sure you hit them somewhere."

Then the incoming fire began, to devastating effect. It seemed to be passing over the defender's head, but then exploded, showing them with shrapnel. Within seconds each of the defending soldiers was wounded to some extent, though not badly enough to prevent fighting back. And fight back they did. But skill and bravery proved to be no match for the vastly superior firepower of the invaders.

First to fall was Pte. Pearson, a young man barely out of basic training. One of the exploding rounds turned his head into a colander oozing blood, brains, and shattered bone.

MCpl. DuBois cursed and tossed a grenade. His aim was true and it hit the wall and bounced behind the curve in the corridor. The resulting explosion elicited some muffled screams, and a black helmet rolled messily towards the defenders leaving a red trail behind it.

Shots were exchanged for a time. Then a smallish object came sailing toward the defenders and landed behind the barricade. Pte. Wong ran forward, picked it up, and hurled it back toward the attackers. But this action exposed him to direct fire, and the enemy took advantage of his lack of cover. The resulting storm of bullets briefly created a red mist around the soldier, who then crumbled lifeless to the ground. But his sacrifice was not in vain, as the invader's own grenade exploded to deadly effect amongst its original owners. Combat body armour, no matter how modern, is no match for the shrapnel emitted by modern explosives detonated at close range.

This explosion created a brief lull in the fighting. DuBois signaled his remaining soldiers to reload their weapons, if they were still able. Within seconds the firing from the invaders resumed.

* * *

Pte. Goldstein had a plan. A short distance from the computer room was a security weapons locker. It was locked, but the electronic lock was not much of problem. Especially since he and his friend had figured out how to open it some months ago, as a way to stave off the boredom of their assignment. He took out a pair of shotguns, ammunition on belts, and large green box. He rummaged around looking for something else but without finding what he was looking for. The time weighed heavily on him, so he headed back to the computer room with his bounty.

"OK, Jase, here's a couple of shotguns. Even *we* can hit something with these," declared Pte. Goldstein.

"Great idea! But what's the box for?" queried his friend. Then he saw the look on Goldstein's face and felt himself go white, "Is that what I think it is?"

"Yah," said Goldstein sadly, "A thermobaric area denial grenade. Although how anyone could call something the size of a laser printer a 'grenade' is beyond me."

"Did you bring along the remote detonator? The manual may claim those things are 'directional', but the kill radius is fucking insane. Please tell me you brought the remote detonator," pleaded Philips.

Pte. Goldstein just shook his head, his eyes tearing up.

"That's OK, Sam," sighed Pte. Philips, "The only important thing is to make them pay a damn high price for this. That's the only important thing now. We'll set up the TADG to aim down the hall, then set up a barricade to hide it. We can enfilade them from either end of barricade. Better set up a dead-man switch for the TADG while we're at it, too."

The sounds of distant gunfire and explosions could be heard clearly.

"The hostiles have hit the intersection. Won't be long now," said Pte. Goldstein, wiping his eyes.

The two of them got to work quickly but efficiently. They were Canadian soldiers, and they knew their duty

* * *

The mood in the Treasure Vault was sombre. The faint thud of explosions had stopped. A quick check of the security scanner showed that the hostiles were on the move again. Fewer in number, but still moving towards them.

"OK," said Yancey quietly, "So what do we do now?"

Cpl. Fleming looked thoughtfully at the security readouts, "We have some time yet. They appear to be moving more slowly, and with about half their original number. That's good. Maybe some of their equipment got destroyed, too, but we can't count on that. Assuming they're still coming here, their path has a few twists and turns. The only major facility between us and them is the computer room. But that's manned by a couple of computer geeks, not real soldiers. Can't imagine how they could do anything to stop the hostiles."

"One thing about this doesn't make sense," said Simon in a puzzled tone.

"Only one?" Pte. Landry gently teased.

Simon blushed but continued, "Well, we've got a force of troops hitting us hard to break in. And we're assuming that the target is the contents of the Treasure Vault. So how were they planning to get it all out? They either blow it in place, and that makes no sense, or they carry it out to transport elsewhere. So where are the extra bodies and equipment needed to carry everything out?"

The two soldiers looked at each other in alarm.

"Oh shit," said Fleming, "That means there's more of them coming. A lot more."

* * *

"All lined up, Sam?"

"Yeah. Got your shotgun loaded with killshot rounds?"

"Yep. Hah - imagine if Sgt Jansen from Basic could see us now? Locked, loaded, and wearing bandoleers of shells."

"Heh. We're a right pair of frickin' Level 60 hard-asses, we are. Wait - security sensors show Bad Guys coming up just beyond the bend. Safety off, friend."

"Safety off. Its been an honour serving with you Private Goldstein."

"The honour has been mine, Private Phillips."

A shadow moved on the curve of the corridor and a black-suited figure began to appear. Pte. Jansen fired his shotgun. The bulk of the shot went wide, but several of the large deadly pellets hit the target. They heard a soft grunt and the figure stumbled back.

Jansen turned to say something to his friend, but Pte. Goldstein's shotgun bellowed and Jansen turned and fired without thinking, and the shadowy figures retreated. But only for a second. Then several figures leapt out and fired a continuous stream of bullets at the makeshift barricade. The barricade melted under the impacts, and the air above became a fog of exploding shrapnel. The shotguns each fired once more, then became silent.

* * *

"The security system shows that the hostiles paused briefly near the computer room, but they're still coming," said Cpl. Fleming, "What I can't understand is why there are fewer of them."

"Maybe the 'computer geeks' were better soldiers than you gave them credit for," said Simon quietly.

"Maybe, and ... wait! More hostiles! One, two, no, three groups entering the Palace. And they're moving fast! Really fast! Must have mechanized transport of some sort. And there are lots of them! Almost in range of the remaining security cams!" shouted Cpl. Fleming.

"Time's run out, babe. It's our turn. We've got to neutralize the hellbombs," whispered Pte. Landry.

"What do you mean 'neutralize'?" asked Yancey, although he began to suspect what the answer was going to be.

160

Cpl. Fleming's face was a study in granite, "The bio weapons are pretty easy to neutralize. The bugs may be weaponized, but the containers aren't. Just break the casings and let the bugs leak out. The nukes are a lot tougher problem. Those *are* fully functional weapons, complete with tough casings and failsafe mechanisms."

Yancey asked, "But won't simply releasing the bugs be enough? With the nukes thoroughly contaminated, they can't be transported. Can they?"

"Yance, we're dealing with the Sword of Infinity Ascending here. They'll sacrifice anyone or anything to get the job done," Simon pointed out.

"Exactly," said Pte. Landry softly, "That means we need to crack open the nukes, extract the fissile material and shatter it into many small pieces. That way the hostiles won't have time to collect more than a small amount of anything. They're on the clock here, and can't stay too long. It's essentially a 'Long Watch' scenario."

Yancey understood the reference, understood the consequences, and queried, "How can we help?"

Simon looked at his friend with a puzzled look on his face.

The two soldiers waved off the offer to help, and turned away to begin gathering the necessary equipment.

"Simon, it's from an old science fiction story by Robert Heinlein," began Yancey, "He posited a central repository of nuclear weapons on the moon, manned by a multinational force, aimed at the Earth to preserve the peace. Sort of a UN with teeth. Anyways, one day some officers decide that they'd make better rulers than elected leaders so they stage a coup. One of the bomb tech officers gets wind of this, decides that it is wrong, and locks himself in the bomb room. Problem is, the Bad Guys will be able to eventually cut their way in. So the hero decides that the only way to neutralize the threat is to disable the missiles, which he does. Then he realizes that a bomb delivery mechanism isn't too hard to cobble together, and that he's got to neutralize the bombs themselves. And the only way to do that is to open each bomb, remove the fissionable material, and break it into too many pieces to be usable as bomb stuff."

"Yancey, what happens to the officer?" Simon asked quietly.

"Uhm, he dies from radiation poisoning. He buys enough time for outside forces to stop the coup, but is fully aware of the price he'll have to pay."

"Well that sucks," said Simon with feeling as he turned to the two soldiers, "But like Yancey says, how can we help?"

Just then a low-pitched *boom* briefly filled the room and their bodies, more felt than heard. All the lights and the computer displays went out briefly, then came back on. They turned towards the security camera monitors and saw a sea of roiling white and yellow.

Cpl. Fleming ran to the security display and frantically began punching buttons.

"Oh shit oh shit oh shit," he chanted as he worked quickly but carefully. Then he paused and stood erect, "The geeks must have got their hands on a TADG and detonated it!"

"A who what?" an excited but puzzled Yancey asked.

Pte. Landry explained, "A thermobaric area denial grenade. Think of it as something like a claymore mine, but creating a pressure wave rather than shrapnel."

"Uhmm," interjected Simon, "Don't those things work by using the oxygen in the air to produce the pressure wave? Claymore mines are directional, aren't they? How can this tadgee thingie be directional?"

"Well, directional-ish," admitted Pte. Landry, "They're supposed to be detonated with a remote detonator for that very reason. Very new, very deadly. In a building like this with strong-walled corridors to channel the blast, well..."

Cpl. Fleming interjected, "Sorry to interrupt, love, but security sensors are detecting movement. Faint, but definite. Looks like only a few hostiles, and they're on foot. Heading this way. Slowly, but moving."

He paused for a moment, looking intently at the displays.

"We've got a dozen nukes to neutralize and a couple dozen racks of bio hell to smash. If we can get a few minutes to work, then the two of us can do this."

He looked longingly at Pte. Landry, seeing all the might-have-beens that would now be lost. "There's no time to put on the isolation suits, so we'll be going in dressed as we are. But that's OK, the suits would have just slowed us down."

He turned towards the civilians, "Molly and I will go in, and move the crates of bio-hell around the nukes."

"But how will you neutralize the nukes?" puzzled Simon.

"We use their built-in failsafe mechanisms," said Landry with a sad smile.

"Uhm, I read somewhere that those failsafe mechanisms were designed to explode with considerable force, to shatter and scatter the fissionable material," said Yancey.

"Exactly," said Fleming as he stepped forward. He drew his pistol and handed it to Yancey. Landry drew hers and handed it to Simon.

Fleming continued, "We go in and open up the casings. That part is pretty easy, but it activates that final failsafe you mentioned. We wire up them up to a large battery, throw the switch, and the failsafe circuits will detect that

163

as an attempted breach and blow the charges. Detonating the failsafe charges of all the nukes will make for a pretty large explosion, but the vault door should be strong enough to contain it. Enough of the bio hell will survive to fully contaminate the entire sealed room. Now you two are going to walk out of here and we're going to lock the vault door behind you. There's enough damage to the structure for you to find ways around the hostiles. If you're lucky. It's not much of a chance, but it's all I can offer to you right now. Don't argue, just go and let us do our duty."

With that the two soldiers grabbed Yancey and Simon and forcibly ejected them from the vault, then closed the door.

* * *

While Fleming had been explaining to the civilians, Landry had been getting the airlock prepped for their final trip into the storage chamber. After ejecting the two civilians, the soldiers jogged to the airlock and passed through as quickly as they could.

Fleming moved the crates of the bio weapons into position while Landry quickly opened up the rear access door of each of the nuclear bombs. He helped her to attach wires to each bomb's inner access hatches, then ran a wire to the battery box.

"What do you think of the chances for the civilians, Doug?" inquired Pte. Landry as she worked quickly.

"Slim to none, Molly. But we've done all that we can for them. Hand me those pliers, will you?" replied Cpl. Fleming.

They heard the door to the vault begin to open. Black-covered figures raced in, and saw Fleming and Landry in the inner chamber. Some rushed towards the airlock, only to find it locked. Others aimed their weapons at the window separating the two rooms.

"Are you ready, my love?" Fleming asked.

"For you, always, my love," Landry replied.

Automatic weapons roared at the armoured glass separating the invaders from the defenders, and a spiderweb of cracks began to form.

The two defenders completed the electrical circuit, and the wires glowed red as the battery quickly discharged.

Their long watch ended.

CHAPTER EIGHTEEN
Bear Trap

Yancy and Simon left the room and the door locked automatically as it shut. They turned towards the corridor and stared aghast at the scene. The corridor had been transformed into a blackened caricature of its previous rundown, but relatively clean, glory. Only a few of the lights were working, and even they were flickering. They could feel a breeze as air rushed in to fill the partial vacuum left by the TADG.

"Which way?" inquired Simon, hesitantly.

"Let's just go up the corridor for now, towards the exit," replied Yancey, "But carefully. We don't want to run into any those Sword crazies."

They continued to exit as quickly and quietly as they could. When they came to the remains of the Computer Room, they had to pause to figure out a way around the devastation that greeted them.

"OK," said Yancey quietly, "I think now is the time to make a dogleg. The remains of the Sword teams will be along soon enough, and we need to stay out of their sight. How about if we go into the Computer Room? I can see breaks in the wall and the one beyond it, so that is probably our best chance."

Simon just nodded, and the two gingerly entered the room and came to a horrified halt at the sight of blackened pieces of what had once been human. Gulping frantically, they continued towards the gap in wall. When they reached it, they carefully peered around the edges and saw no sign of the hostile forces, just another hole in the opposite wall. They had just crossed over into the next room when the sound of purposeful movement reached their ears. Ducking behind debris they waited with trepidation as the sounds moved down the corridor towards them, and then past them towards the Vault. Yancey and Simon waited for a few seconds, but the urgency of their need to escape drove them onward. They crossed the room, opened the door at the other end, and carefully peered out. The hostile forces had by this time moved far enough to be around the bend of the corridor, so the two friends slipped out and continued towards the exit.

* * *

Colonel Brown was not a happy soldier. He had, in his opinion, deserted his post. Under orders by a superior officer and in the face of a seemingly superior force to be sure, but it still left the taste of ashes in his mouth. At least that fool, General TwoTee, had stopped running. Fortunately Col. Brown had kept control of his own forces, and they were still together as a small but effective force.

"OK, Major," Brown said to his second-in-command, "Give me the sitrep."

"Yessir," said Major Frontenac, his breath streaming in the cold air, "The scouts have reported that the bulk of the hostiles have entered the Palace, leaving a half-dozen vehicles outside with about a dozen troops left to guard them. The troops are all wearing that high-tech armour of theirs, and and all armed with those fancy rifles. Plus a couple of them look to be toting grenade launchers of some sort. Might be hand-held mortars, for all we can tell."

He paused a moment then continued briskly, "Our own troops have their M-16's or pistols. A couple of them have 50-cal sniping rifles, but not many rounds. We've picked up all of our stragglers, and I don't think there's going to be any more coming out."

Frontenac finished his report, paused and then licked his lips quickly before continuing, "Sir, what are we going to do?"

"Ever read about how they used to trap bears before firearms were invented?" smiled Col. Brown.

Maj. Frontenac kept his face still. He'd heard the Colonel ramble on about such things far too many times over the past year. "No sir," was all he said.

"Not surprised," continued Brown, "They'd find a hole in a tree or big log and hammer in some spikes, with the points facing away from the hole. Then they'd smear a bunch of raw meat or honey inside the hole and wait for a bear to show up. The bear would come, shove in his paw, but because of the way the spikes faced it couldn't get the paw out again. So this big, bad animal that could crush any number of mere humans was now trapped and unable to use its strength against the humans, who could now attack it in relative safety. And that's how our ancestors took care of bears. Now it's our turn, my young Major."

Col. Brown thought for a moment, then issued his orders, "I want snipers on top of those ridges between us and the forces at the Palace. They're only at the main portal, so we don't have to worry about flankers ... but send out a couple scouts to keep an eye out anyways.

Gather our troops and disperse them so we can focus our fire on the hostiles. Then take a squad and dig in where I show you. I've got to go and make sure that General TwoTee doesn't interfere with our counterattack, then I'll be back here ASAP. Plan the attack to start in 10 minutes."

They both smiled hungrily.

* * *

Inside the Treasure Vault of the Shattered Palace, three black-clad figures struggled to their feet. One of them had blood leaking from several gashes, but the other two appeared unharmed. They slowly looked around and saw only debris and destruction. They looked into the formerly sealed chamber and saw only a roiling cloud rising up towards them from the Treasure Vault.

They turned towards the door that had been shut by the force of the explosion and began trying to open it. The figure with the damaged suit began to twitch, then stagger, and then fall. Within seconds the Sword soldier's body heaved as if vomiting, but the helmet's tinted shield hid what lay within. The soldier began clawing at his helmet, trying with desperate motions to pull it off. The efforts quickly became less and less forceful, even as his body writhed. Finally the soldier lay still, as tendrils of fog rose to cover the body.

The other two Sword soldiers made obeisance over the body of their fallen comrade and continued their efforts. Finally they managed to get the door open and began to exit, stepping carefully over the debris.

One of the soldiers slipped, and caught his leg on a sharp piece of debris, slashing open a wound on his thigh. The other soldier turned to his comrade, and they stood there silently facing each other. The injured soldier bowed his head and opened his arms. His comrade walked to him and clasped his shoulders. The injured soldier then pulled out his knife and offered it. The uninjured soldier took it, and without hesitation plunged it into the other's neck. As his comrade fell, the remaining soldier made obeisance, then turned and walked on.

Within a few meters his path was blocked by one of the automatic safety doors. The soldier brushed the dust off the control panel, and taking a device from his belt held it against the control panel. As lights blinked on his device, he pressed buttons on the control panel. Shortly, the door opened, and he could see that this was the only safety door that was still activated. He stepped through and then stopped as another built-in instrument buzzed softly in his suit. He examined the instrument, and his shoulders sagged. The suits were not as impervious as was expected, even when unpunctured. He took a grenade from his belt, activated it, then bowed his head. There were none left to make obeisance over his body.

The fog rose, covering the Sword soldiers, then roiled forth unimpeded down the corridors.

* * *

Yancey and Simon could see the portal, and were running down the corridor towards it. They paused for breath, panting as quietly as they could. Then they heard a loud explosion from behind them, then silence. A few heartbeats later the silence was broken was the shriek of pressurized air escaping its containment.

"That can't be good," breathed Simon, "They blew the Vault, but if that sound is what I think it is, then the Bad Stuff is coming out and heading this way. Time to boogie, Yance."

"Agreed," said Yancey, "Check your pistol."

He had to show Simon how to prepare the pistol for firing and take the safety off, then he prepared his own.

"We've only each got one clip of bullets, so don't waste 'em. Don't hesitate to shoot, but don't waste shots. You set?"

Simon nodded.

The both darted out through the portal door, and outside. The fresh air felt good!

Then they saw the vehicles parked there and the black-clad figures standing there transfixed by the sounds of the explosions. Simon and Yancey froze for a moment then moved as quickly as they could along the curve of the outside wall, hoping to escape unseen. Bullets chipping at the wall around them made it clear that they had been detected. The two now ran as quickly as they could to put the curve of the wall between themselves and their attackers. They ran towards the road, towards the trees that were scattered between the building and road, glancing over their shoulders as they ran.

But a race between out-of-shape civilians and trained soldiers can only end one way. Just as they reached one of the trees on the way to the roadway, Yancey and Simon saw a pair of Sword soldiers come around the building towards them. Yancey and Simon spun around, and using the tree for cover, squatted down, and aimed their pistols at the enemy soldiers.

* * *

"Colonel Brown, what is the meaning of this?" a familiar belligerent voice brayed.

Col. Brown turned to face the General, "Sir, we're setting up a defensive line against the hostiles."

Brown turned to Major Frontenac and nodded, "Carry on, Major," then turned to face the General.

"Sir, we have a small force of hostiles plus vehicles at the front of the main portal. I have an effective force capable of responding to the intrusion, and I ... "

All discussion was interrupted by a loud, strident pattern of *whoops* and *warbles* coming from the Palace.

"Oh, shit," breathed Brown, then in a stronger voice continued, "The Vault has been breached! We MUST shut the portal door before the contamination reaches the outside!"

The face of General Thomas Thansworth the Third went from flushed red to white. "NO! We must evacuate this area immediately! The important thing is for us to report back to Headquarters what has happened here! Any contamination can be taken care of by a high-altitude saturation bombing of the area. Napalm and thermobaric weapons will sufficiently cleanse the area ... we can call it a training accident or something. But we MUST evacuate and report!"

Col. Brown looked around at the crisp clean wilderness. He took a deep breath of the sweet-smelling air and exhaled, "Yessir. I ordered a communications crew to set up just over that ridge. They should be set up by now, so you should go over there and order in the evac and cleanup strike. I'll go tell Major Frontenac to recall the men and initiate an orderly retreat."

General Thansworth sniffed disapprovingly but nodded and began stomping towards the indicated ridge. Col. Brown watched him go for a moment then turned and trotted in the direction Major Frontenac had gone.

While this exchange was going on, Major Frontenac was kneeling by a sniper who had signaled for his attention. "OK, Corporal, what have you got?"

"Sir," the corporal briskly said without taking his eye from the scope, "I've got those two civilians who warned us about the attack exiting the Palace and being pursued by two hostiles. The civilians ran but the hostiles are about to catch up to them. Orders, sir?"

Frontenac thought quickly. Everyone was in position, and the Colonel would be here shortly. And they did owe the civilians something. "Do you have a clean shot against the hostiles?"

"Yessir."

"Then take the bastards out."

The sniper's rifle barked once, paused briefly to chamber another round, then barked again. Armoured they might have been, but a 50-caliber bullet to the base of the neck will not be stopped by mere body armour. The black-clad figures dropped.

Just then, Col. Brown jogged up. "Did you decide to start without me?" he inquired with a grim smile.

"No sir," said Major Frontenac, "But two hostiles were about to kill the two civilians who warned us about the attack. Didn't think you'd want that to happen, sir."

"Quite right," said Brown crisply, "Well the fat's in the fire so let's carry on, shall we? We don't have much time."

The battle to re-take the Shattered Palace began.

* * *

Yancey and Simon clenched their fingers and their pistols barked once, twice. To their surprise the Sword soldiers chasing them collapsed.

They looked with stunned disbelief at the two dead soldiers, then at each other.

"I think I'm going to be sick," said Simon, his pale face showing a distinct greenish tinge.

Yancey's face clearly showed his agreement with his friend, but he simply said, "Yah, but we've got to get out of here. Like right freakin' *now*, before their friends show up!"

Before Simon could answer, they heard the staccato hammering of gunfire from the direction of the portal door. And the answering *thrum* of the guns of the Sword. Battle had been joined, and this was no place for civilians. So Yancey and Simon turned and kept running down the rough road, away from the battle.

* * *

"Make sure to make every shot count, men!" yelled Col. Brown while firing his own weapon.

But their shots seemed to be having little effect. Several of the Sword soldiers had fallen, but the rest managed to zig and zag out of the line-of-sight of the high-powered sniper rifles. At this range, their body armour was an effective protection against the rifles of the Canadians. But the weapons of the Sword had a much longer effective range, and they had ammunition to spare. Several of the Canadian soldiers had already been slaughtered by those dangerously effective guns.

"Fall back! Fall back!" the order came, and the Canadians fell back. Quickly but in good order, and firing as they went, but beaten back by the Sword.

The Sword, knowing that this was their chance to eliminate the enemy, advanced as the Canadians retreated. Their deadly weapons belched a hailstorm of death at the retreating Canadians. No more of of the Sword fell, but several more Canadian soldiers perished. The Sword was an inexorable black-clad tide of death that was steadily pushing the Canadians ever back.

The Sword pushed the Canadians back over the ridge from which they had come, firing volleys of bullets and grenades. Then over the top they went and saw the Canadians in full retreat. They raised their weapons to dispose of the cowardly enemy. And then all hell broke loose.

Canadian soldiers burst out of the snow to either side of them just a few tens of meters away, and with rapid but controlled firing began hosing the Sword with bullets. Round after round, dozens of bullets hit each of the Sword soldiers. Body armour will stop a bullet penetrating, and even dissipate the force of the impact somewhat, but even obsolete military rifles will fire a bullet that hits with tremendous kinetic energy. Especially when fired at such close range. The soldiers of the Sword were not so much 'shot' as bludgeoned by the impact of the rain of bullets. Only one was killed by a bullet penetrating his armour. The rest died as every bone in their body was broken and every internal organ repeatedly beaten to uselessness.

Within a handful of brutal seconds, the battle was over.

* * *

Even as the soldiers of the Sword were slaughtered, Colonel Brown had turned around and run towards the ridge, followed by his troops. Even above the din of battle he heard the alarms of the Palace screaming out their warning of impending doom. He knew that if he didn't get the portal door closed, the deadly brew of nuclear and bio-warfare hell would escape and contaminate the entire area. Probably for generations.

"To the portal! To the portal!" he cried as continued his desperate race, "We've got to close the portal door!"

He sped by Major Frontenac who kneeling by a downed Canadian soldier. "Secure the area!" Brown yelled as he sped by. He should stay and supervise, he knew, but the only thing that he could focus on was the thought of the deadly brew about to spew forth from within the Palace.

Within a minute he had reached the portal and its door. Some of the younger troops were already there. A sergeant had taken charge and was directing one set of soldiers to push against the door, and another to check the manual closing mechanism. The soldiers pushing were having no effect.

Col. Brown ran up and skidded to a stop. "Report!" he gasped out. The screaming of the alarms was almost deafening.

"Sir!" yelled the sergeant, "Power to the door is out, and the door is too heavy to push closed. I've got men opening up the manual closing mechanism ... wait, they have it open and are cranking away!"

Brown looked and saw the young soldiers frantically heaving away on a crankshaft-shaped rod that had inserted into a geared mechanism. The door was slowly swinging shut! But the manual mechanism was on the inside. To close the door would require that those turning the crank to stay inside as the door closed.

Just then, Major Frontenac ran up, gasping for breath. "Sir ... " he began.

"No time, Jean," said Col. Brown as he opened his coat, "Here are the station logs, my last report, and all the security data that I could grab."

He thrust a large brown envelope into Frontenac's hands, "You have command. Don't take any shit from that asshole TwoTee, either. My report makes it clear that this was all his fault. Thank you for everything."

And with that he ran into the Palace, grabbed one of the young soldiers and roughly threw him outside the door. "You have a wife and children. You're dismissed."

And he began turning the crank.

Through the haze of exhaustion he saw the other young soldiers tossed outside and new bodies take their place.

He forced his eyes to focus, and saw the familiar faces of the Last Leggers.

"Ten seconds on, then ten seconds off," bawled an elderly sergeant, "SWITCH!"

Col. Brown was roughly shoved aside as another elderly soldier took his place. Brown panted heavily. The door was closing!

"SWITCH!"

Brown resumed his place on the crankshaft and pumped along with the others, his lungs labouring and his arms beginning to burn.

"SWITCH!"

Brown relinquished his place thankfully. He glanced at the door, and saw that it was almost closed. Then he looked down the corridor and saw a fog creeping towards them. The alarms almost drowned out the drumming of his heart and the sounds as he and the others greedily sucked in air.

"SWITCH!"

Brown again resumed his place at the crankshaft and pumped away, his strength almost gone. Suddenly the crankshaft jammed and the labouring soldiers stumbled and collapsed. As one, they turned to the door and saw that it was closed.

Col. Brown slowly got to his feet, lungs labouring, head bent with exhaustion.

"TEN-SHUT!" a voice yelled.

Brown lifted his head and saw the soldiers of the Last Leggers standing at parade attention, their arms lifted in a perfect military salute. Although each of them was soaked in sweat and breathing in gasps, Brown thought that they were the most beautiful sight that he'd seen in a very long time. He faced them, braced to attention, and returned their salute as the fog swirled about their feet. Then their legs.

And in a very few minutes, the Shattered Palace became a tomb.

* * *

Outside, Major Jean Frontenac watched as the door closed. Then he turned as his subordinates returned from their examination of the Sword soldiers. Most were carrying weapons of some sort. "What have you found?" he inquired sharply.

The reporting soldiers had been gazing inquiringly at the closing door and shrieking alarms from within, but seeing that the Major was glaring at them waiting for his report, training took over and they summarized what they had found. The Sword weapons were of an advanced version that included lock-out mechanisms … not biometric, but requiring some sort of encoded key to make them function. There were two types of weapons, the advanced rifle, and some sort of missile launcher.

The door closed with a *thump* and silence descended as the shrieking of the alarms was cut off. Frontenac gazed at the closed door for a second, then turned to his troops and was about to speak when another group of soldiers ran up. Frontenac recognized one of them as being the American corporal, Jamison. He pointed at the captured weapons and asked if he recognized them.

Cpl. Jamison roughly grabbed one of each type out of the hands of the Canadian soldiers and shook them at the Major. "These here are the most advanced weapons our country has made. Don't rightly know now those God-forsaken hostiles got their filthy hands on 'em, but by Jesus these are pure death!"

"Can we make use of them?" inquired Frontenac.

"Hell, no!" exclaimed Jamison, "These are programmed

to be useless to anyone without the proper passkey. And those passkeys must be used by a specific, living, breathing soldier. And you just killed all those terrorist sons-a-bitches. These here are now just clubs, as far as you-all are concerned. Ain't no way on God's sweet earth for the built-in security to be bypassed. Not by you lot, at any rate."

"Sir! We've got incoming aircraft. Two of them. Look like choppers of some sort! No IFF!" yelled one of the Canadian soldiers gazing intently at a hand-held screen.

"Sergeant Brighton, front and centre," said Frontenac briskly.

The named sergeant trotted up and saluted.

Frontenac grabbed the weapons from Jamison's hands and handed them to the sergeant. "We've got incoming and we need to be able to use these."

"Yessir," said the sergeant, "Won't take but a minute."

And he began opening them up and poking at them with tools that he pulled from within his jacket.

"Hold on there, chief," spluttered Jamison, "Are you deaf? I just told you that those weapons cannot be operated by anyone other than authorized personnel. And ain't none of us authorized!"

"Done sir," said the sergeant, "Did you want me to fix the others?"

"As quickly as possible, and pass them around as we discussed," said the Major, "Corporals Thickson and Slade, front and centre!"

The two named corporals trotted up. Frontenac presented the two with the adjusted weapons. "We've got two incoming helicopters. Take them out."

Just then, the helicopters in question could be seen just above the trees, with just a whisper of sound coming from them. "Their sound suppression system is really very good," Major Frontenac thought to himself.

"Take them out gentlemen, if you please," he said out loud.

The two corporals pointed their newly-acquired weapons at the helicopters and began firing. A heartbeat later two other captured weapons began firing, and the regular weapons joined in. One helicopter managed to fire a single missile, but that was intercepted and destroyed before it got very far. The debris of its explosion fell not far from the debris of the helicopters.

The attack on the Shattered Palace was over.

CHAPTER NINETEEN
Judgement Of The Apostles

The room was austere to the point of bleakness. A circular wooden table, of great age, sat in the centre. A dozen high-backed chairs of a simple ancient design were equally spaced about the table. An single additional chair sat carefully placed off to one side, halfway between the wall and the table.

The twelve men around the table were dressed in simple black, loose-fitting clothing. The only sign of adornment was a knotted cord at one shoulder, each of a different design and colour. Their mood was sombre, but with an element of anticipation.

One of the group spoke with a harsh voice that was not loud, but was clearly heard by all.

"I am Apostle One, and I speak for Infinity Ascending. I will receive the report of Apostle Five on the results of the mission to acquire the weapons of power."

The man known as Apostle Five stood and made obeisance. "I regret to inform The Council that the mission to obtain the nuclear and biological weapons from the facility known as the Shattered Palace has failed."

The harsh voice spoke again, "And what was the cause of this failure? Much effort was expended to arrange for the American security contingent to be neutralized. The remaining military force was composed of mere Canadians, and most of those either of retirement age or of poor quality. Was the Sword contaminated by lack of faith? By fear? Was the information and instrumentation that we provided you inadequate to the task? Speak!"

Apostle Five stood quietly, showing no sign of emotion except for a single drop of sweat slowly moving down the back of his neck. "No, Apostle One. The Sword did not fail through fear or lack of faith. The information and instrumentation that you provided was adequate to the task. As you predicted, all but a handful of low-ranking Canadian soldiers evacuated the facility. But somehow that handful, although eventually eliminated, managed to destroy all the weapons before we could secure them. The interior of the facility is now sealed and contaminated beyond reclamation. None of the Sword survived. Full details and sensor readings have been made available."

The single bead of sweat was joined by another.

The harsh voice was silent for a handful of heartbeats before speaking again, "No operation can be assured of success. I hold the Sword blameless for the failure of the mission, though this is a serious setback for our plans to follow The Path."

Although no-one moved, a sense of relief was evident amoungst the assembled. And even more so, a sense of pride reaffirmed. Like a group of attack dogs being praised by their master.

"And yet," continued the harsh voice, "I cannot abide the fear that has come to infest this Council of Apostles. You, Apostle Five, show the signs of fear and lack of faith. You have allowed yourself to become infected, and this has affected your judgment and abilities. Fear and lack of faith cause weakness, and not one of us can be allowed to have our faith weakened in our journey along The Path. You are a contagion that must be cleansed. Brothers, I command you to do your duty and cleanse this contamination. In the name of our Order."

Without hesitation, eleven guns were drawn and aimed at the man called Apostle Five.

"I have served our Order my entire life," Apostle Five said evenly, his voice strong and unwavering, "I have served as an acolyte, as a member of the Sword, and as an apostle on the Council. My devotion to The Path has not wavered."

He paused and made obeisance. "My life is for our Order," he said simply, his head bowed.

"Your devotion is noted, but so too is your contamination. You have failed your test. Execute him."

As one, eleven guns fired and the man called Apostle Five crumbled to the floor, blood pooling around his body.

The harsh voice spoke again, "All ranks from twelve to six will be increased by one. Choose a new apostle to become 'Apostle Twelve' from amoungst the ranks of the Sword. I leave the choice to you. That is the first task of your new ranks, and your first test. Report to me when your choice is made."

With that, the man called Apostle One strode towards the exit. Three of the others followed behind him.

Those remaining stood motionless for a moment, then made obeisance to the back of the one called Apostle One. Then each removed his cord and passed it down to the next in line. The last placed his on the table in front of an empty chair. One of them took the cord from the cooling corpse and attached it to his shoulder. He looked dispassionately at his former colleague.

"We shall now select a new Brother to join us. But

before we begin - Apostle Eleven, would you please call housekeeping and have them clean up this refuse?"

Thus purified of weakness, the Council of Apostles for Infinity Ascending began their deliberations.

CHAPTER TWENTY
Rise Again

The Busted Flush thrummed happily as it rolled down the highway. Yancey was careful to keep it at the posted limit. The last thing he wanted was to get pulled over. The police would probably get upset about the pistols that he and Simon had tossed into the back seat. And the blood staining their shirts. Not to mention the strained and haunted look in their eyes.

In their desperate flight down the roadway they had literally stumbled into a Sword soldier as he came around a large boulder. Whether the soldier was a scout or fleeing from the battle they didn't know, and it really didn't matter. As all three collapsed into a heap of tangled limbs and weapons, all that mattered was surviving. The Sword soldier fought silently and efficiently, striking out with his rifle and well-placed blows from his hands and feet. Yancy had landed near the soldier's head, so he rolled over on top of the him and pinned the head and arms as best he could. Simon, who was being kicked, had a momentary reprieve. He took advantage of it to jump on the soldier's chest, jam his pistol into the neck, and pointing upwards into the helmet pulled the trigger. The blast of the pistol was echoed by a ringing as the bullet briefly ricocheted around inside the armoured helmet. A stream of red liquid, mostly blood but with white flecks, was forced out of the initial opening and sprayed both Yancey and Simon. They must have both shut down emotionally for a bit, because they both came to their senses as they ran up to the Busted Flush. They dug it out of its concealment, hopped in, and drove away as fast as they could until they exited onto a regular road. Neither had spoken since they had fought the Sword soldier.

The two friends continued along in the thickening silence for a time. The daylight faded into dusk, and Yancey switched on the headlights.

Simon spoke first, "So what do we do now? Who can we go to?"

Yancey quietly replied, "I don't know. It's not like we can trust anyone - not after what we've learned. What we've seen. If the wrong people learn of our existence, we're liable to be tossed into 'protective custody' for any number of reasons, or simply made to disappear. The security types would freak about our knowing about the Shattered Palace, for one thing. The security types of *several* nations. Then there's the other players, both powers and dominions."

Simon thought about this for a minute, then spoke with a vehemence that Yancey had never heard, "We can't stand by and do nothing, Yance. Those 'powers and dominions' as you call them are using our country ... using all of *us* ... as pawns in their fucking power games. They've turned Canada into a battleground as they suck us dry. We can't just sit back and watch. *I* can't sit back and do nothing." Simon paused, then continued pleadingly "But what can we *do*?"

"I know what you mean, Simon. *They* hold all the aces. *They* have all the power. It's not as simple as taking out

186

this or that person. I wish to hell it was. They've gamed and corrupted the entire system, the entire governing infrastructure. Not everyone, of course, but enough."

He paused briefly then continued "And we've got to find Gretchen. She's one of the few leads that we've got, and our friend."

Once again, the silence between them grew.

Finally Yancey heaved a great sigh and said with conviction, "But we will fight them. Infinity Ascending, their Sword, the corrupted, and all the other powers and dominions. Somehow. We will stand and hold. We will endure. We're Canadians, and that's what we do."

The night enveloped them as they raced through the darkness into an uncertain future.

Sneak Preview
Darkness Comes Reaping

Book 2 in the *Ascending Darkness* series.

It was the sound that got his attention when awareness returned to him. A soft meaty thudding that sounded vaguely familiar. Then came the feeling of a sharp twisting movement. It puzzled him at first, then he realized that the former always seemed to precede the latter. Following the movement came a sensation of pressure, building quickly to a dull pain that spread from the point where the pressure had occurred. He fit the pieces together and realized that all of the events were related, somehow, and the process of figuring it out gave him a vague sense of accomplishment. After some indeterminate time the process was repeated. Then again. And again. It gradually occurred to him that not only were all of the event related, but that they were happening to him. Something was hitting him. He tried to think, but the sounds and motion of the repeated blows made it impossible to hold together a chain of coherent reasoning. And he was tired. So tired.

The various sensations stopped, finally, and he felt grateful for the quiet and a chance for his thoughts to coalesce into something vaguely coherent. He became aware that something new was happening, something trying to get his attention. Voices. That was what they were, voices that saying something. He tried to focus his shattered attention on what they were saying - maybe it was important. Everything felt so thick to him, thick and disconnected.

"Mister Franklin" he heard the voice say, over and over again.

This confused him. He didn't know anyone named Mister.

The voice continued its chanting, in a slow melodic manner.

He finally came to the realization that the voice was talking to *him*. With this realization came a limited return of awareness. He had a body, with a head and torso and arms and legs. He had forgotten about them, somehow. And he was lying horizontally on a hard surface, unable to move his arms or legs. The trickle of awareness increased, and memories started coming back to him. Memories of imprisonment and beatings. He was being beaten. Again. But he couldn't remember why. Everything hurt, and he was so tired.

"Mister Franklin" the voice intoned, "The Fist of Tolerance takes no pleasure in these activities. We only seek to guide you to The Path, but we require your assistance. Please, we beg of you, help us to guide you."

Yancey carefully shook his head as if to clear it, and opened his eyes as much as the swollen flesh surrounding them would allow. The bright light cut like a knife, and he quickly shut his eyes again and tried to move his head away. Strong hands firmly held his head, and a cool cloth was placed over his eyes. Yancey made a soft sigh that rustled through dry chapped lips.

"We have dimmed the lights for you, Mister Franklin" intoned the voice, "And we will try to make you comfortable, for a time. You must realize that coming to The Path is inevitable, for it is the will of God that we do so. Each and every one of us. This scourging of the flesh is necessary only because you resist the inevitable. All that is required is for you to confess. Confess and tell us everything that is in your heart. Tell us how you found this place. Tell us where your friends are. Tell us about the Shattered Palace. Confess. Confess and receive God's blessing and forgiveness. Confess and be comforted in body and soul."

Memories started to come back, like a broken mirror reassembling itself. Yancey remembered that he was in the hands of the Sword of Infinity Ascending. He remembered being captured. He remembered the interrogations. Most importantly, he remembered that his friends were now safely away from the Sword. Nothing could force him to betray or endanger them. Nothing. He tried to form words, but his lips refused to cooperate. He felt a moist cloth against his mouth, easing the dryness. The cloth was removed and he tried again to speak. This time his lips worked, or at least well enough to form words.

"Fuck you."

Not many words, and not everything that he wanted to say to his captors, but it would suffice.

He felt the cloth around his eyes being removed, and then felt the heat of the blinding lights returning.

"You have only yourself to blame for this, Mister Franklin" said a deep sad voice, "The Fist of Tolerance exists only to guide sinners back to The Path ordained by God. You are a lost soul, and we will help guide you back to The Path. Remember that as we scourge the flesh."

The beating began again. And as before, his inquisitors were puzzled by the laughter that bubbled out of their captor's mouth before he lapsed into semi-consciousness. Yancey knew something they didn't, and the realization always made him laugh. He knew that the beatings couldn't break him. As a child he had grown up with similar sorts of beatings, and and from long practice knew how to retreat into himself to escape the pain.

Some things never change, he thought just before the kaleidescope of memories claimed him once again.

About The Author

Brian Greiner retired from the software development rat race to take up the carefree life of an author. He lives in Ontario, Canada with his wife and three cats.

For the latest news about this and forthcoming books, or to leave a comment (we love feedback!), check out the author's blog at

www.damnfoolpress.com/BrianGreiner

49488888R00109

Made in the USA
Charleston, SC
25 November 2015